Freckled
and Fourteen

by VIOLA ROWE

Illustrated by Jacqueline Tomes

SCHOLASTIC BOOK SERVICES
NEW YORK • TORONTO • LONDON • AUCKLAND • SYDNEY • TOKYO

To Carolyn

Copyright © 1965 by Viola Rowe. This edition is published by Scholastic Book Services, a division of Scholastic Magazines, Inc., by arrangement with William Morrow and Company.

10th printing ••• • ••• • ••• • • • • • • • • • • • ••• • ••• • ••• • ••• • November 1975

Printed in the U.S.A.

CONTENTS

The Dreamiest

It WAS HAPPENING AGAIN, and Rusty Eastman was furious. A quick glance over her shoulder told her that she and her faithful friend, Geraldine Jones, were being followed. They were being followed by some silly boys. The kind of boys who actually enjoyed going to the parties and dances at their junior high. The kind of boys who couldn't think of anything better to do than whistle at girls and follow them home after school.

Rusty, whose name, much to her sorrow, was really Rosalind, muttered, "The creeps!"

Geraldine, who preferred to be called Jeri, ventured, "They've probably got spring fever."

5

The March breeze was so tame, it scarcely stirred a branch or bush along School Street in the midwestern town of Melville. Rusty handed her books to Jeri, while she pulled off her short plaid coat and slung it over her shoulders. But she dismissed any defense of their followers. "If they had half a brain, they'd be trying out for the baseball team."

Jeri handed back Rusty's books and smiled in agreement. "Or for track, on a day like this."

Rusty hastened to point out, "There's no track or cross-country until high school." Though this was something she felt Jeri really should have known, Rusty corrected her faithful friend politely. After all, Jeri's father wasn't athletic coach at the community high school, as her father was. And so Jeri could not be expected to know as much as she knew about school athletics. Besides, Jeri had only one brother, and Rusty had four.

Thinking of brothers naturally led her thoughts to Alan, the oldest of her four brothers. By mentioning track, Jeri probably was encouraging her to talk about Alan. Bragging about him was what it amounted to. After all, every girl didn't have a brother who had been a star athlete in junior high, and now was a star athlete in his sophomore year in high school. Lately, though, something was wrong somewhere. At times, Alan was so different that she was beginning to wonder if she would ever again have cause to brag about him. This was something she was reluctant to admit, even to Jeri.

The boys who were trailing them were becoming bolder. They were making loud noises that might have been meant to resemble "the wild and terrible cry of Tarzan." Or, Rusty thought disdainfully, the boys were probably stupid enough to think the sounds coming from their lips were Indian love calls.

One boy lifted his voice to a girlish soprano to ask Jeri, "Hey, Jones, what's your hurry?"

"Pretend you don't hear them," Rusty offered consolingly to her faithful friend.

Jeri stole a glance over her shoulder. "One of them is Mickey Gordon." So saying, she giggled.

At that Rusty grabbed her friend's arm. "Come on," she ordered sharply. The expression on Jeri's face disturbed her. And that giggle! For a moment Jeri had looked and sounded almost like Debra Damon, the worst flirt in school. As if any minute now Jeri might gush, as Debra was always gushing, "Oh, isn't he the dreamiest?"

It couldn't really happen, of course. Jeri had better sense than to become a chirp like Debra Damon, she was sure. Just the same, Rusty wanted to get Jeri away from these obnoxious boys.

One of them now blasted like a foghorn, "Hey, Eastman! Hey, Rusty, where did you get that red hair? Out of a bottle?"

For one black moment she was stunned. Then she was filled with wrath. Not because a boy had dared to tease her about the color of her hair. She was used to that. Hadn't it been carroty red all her life? What shook her was being accused of getting it from a bottle. As if she would choose to have this curly carroty mop! As if she wouldn't prefer nice straight dark hair like her brothers'. Anything would be better than what she had!

Almost, but not quite, she turned to yell at the boys, to tell them what she thought of them and their remarks. Just in time she stopped herself. For she knew, of course, that it would only bring on more taunts if she let them see they had disturbed her. That much she knew from battling with her brothers.

So instead she yanked Jeri along with her, just in time to beat the traffic light at the corner where Main Street crossed School Street. Only when they were safely across the busy intersection did she look back to where the boys had been halted by the flow of traffic. To her vast relief she saw that they had turned the corner and were walking toward the business district. With a happy sigh she told Jeri, "Now we can talk in peace."

"They could still cross the street and catch up," Jeri remarked.

Rusty eyed her faithful friend with suspicious impatience. She scarcely noticed Jeri's smooth blond hair, which she usually envied; or the light blue of Jeri's eyes and the paleness of her lashes and brows, or even the fact that not a single freckle marred Jeri's fair skin. Along with Rusty's red hair, her freckles were a source of despair to her. No, at that moment she was thinking of other things. Things such as the word just spoken by Jeri. For surely Jeri had sounded wistful? As if she actually hoped those abominable boys would catch up with them!

Rusty opened her mouth, then closed it again. She was imagining things, she told herself. After almost two years of faithful friendship with Jeri—the almost two years since they'd started junior high together—she should know Jeri better than to be thinking suspicious thoughts about her. "Tell me," she ordered, "what was in Eloise Roberts' slam book. About me."

Jeri hedged. "A boy wrote it. You could tell by the writing, a boy wrote it."

"I don't care," Rusty assured her. "I just

want to know what was written about me."

Slam books were being passed around school a lot these days, and almost anyone who wanted to could record his or her impression of a fellow student. None of the comments were complimentary, Rusty knew, for she had scribbled a few herself. About Debra Damon she had written, "Debra thinks she's Sandburg Junior High's gift to the boys." And about the eighth-grade basketball team her slam was, "They aim where the basket ain't." That one had been pretty clever, she thought.

What she wanted to know was what had been written about her that had brought snickers from those who read it. Someone had snatched the slam book before she could get her hands on it. "Tell me," she insisted.

"Well, it said you were a flapper."

"A flapper?" Rusty puzzled. "You mean like in the olden times?"

"No. It said you are always flapping about something."

Rusty burst into loud laughter. "Always flapping! That's good!"

Jeri smiled, a relieved smile. "Yes. You'll have to admit the boy has a sense of humor."

Abruptly, Rusty stopped laughing. A boy had written about her. And what he had written no longer seemed amusing. A flapper, she thought. Always flapping about something, was she?

Jeri hastened to tell of other slams in Eloise Roberts' book. But Rusty was not listening. She was thinking angrily of the boy who had written about her. The ick! The double ick! A lot he knew! He probably didn't know how to hit a baseball or field a curve or anything. Why, he probably didn't know how to play anything harder than leapfrog!

She became aware of a change in the tone of Jeri's voice, and she roused herself from her angry thoughts to listen to what her faithful friend was saying.

Jeri wasn't saying very much. Mostly she was saying a name. "There's your brother Alan."

Sure enough, there he was, coming from the direction of the high school, toward the corner where they both would turn. Looking at him now, nobody would dream that Alan had been a sickly baby. Rusty couldn't actually remember those times when he'd seemed to be on the verge of death. She did remember times when he was sick. But mostly she remembered how she and Alan had raced each other on their tricycles, and carted each other around in their coaster wagon. And how they had climbed trees and built snow forts, and all but lived out of doors except when forced indoors by parents or by hunger. Many a time they had pounded each other in anger; but when it was time for Alan to go to school, both of them had wept because she was too young to go with him.

Today Alan's cheeks were ruddy with color, and he carried his broad shoulders with the same jaunty air with which he'd worn his basketball uniform in seventh grade, his football uniform in eighth grade, and his baseball uniform as a freshman in high school.

"I thought there was batting practice this after," Rusty remarked uneasily to Jeri.

This year Alan had been showing less and less interest in the school's sports activities. Rusty was sure their father, being the athletic coach, must be upset about this. But so far she had not heard him so much as mention it.

Alan saw her, and held up one hand in a casual salute. As he stepped off the curb, a girl came up and crossed the street with him. The two of them laughed as if at something very funny, though Rusty couldn't imagine what could possibly be that hilarious.

"Ugh!" Rusty moaned. "Another of those chirpy girls. I don't know how Alan puts up with them." She couldn't admit that Alan seemed to like girls as much as they liked him. The very thought was just too much to bear.

At her side, Jeri sighed—a loud, heaving

sigh. As if with her last gasp of breath, Jeri murmured, "Oh, Rusty, he's the dreamiest."

She couldn't believe it. She didn't want to believe it. Not of her best friend Jeri. Her friend who had shared her ideals and, with her, had scorned silly boys who liked to go around with girls, and silly girls who tried to be flirts like Debra Damon.

It was all too evident that her friend was no longer faithful to their ideals. As if to make sure that there could be no mistake about it, Jeri said it again, in a whisper this time, a sighing whisper. "He's the dreamiest, Rusty."

Rusty didn't answer. Boys, she thought in despair. Even Alan was among the enemies now. She must have been born under an unlucky star. Or maybe it was because she was thirteen—an unlucky number, thirteen. Since she'd become thirteen, Alan had changed. And now she'd lost her best friend.

How unlucky could she get?

Another Silly

Rusty MANAGED a polite "Hi" when Alan introduced the girl who had crossed the street with him. She was small, with deep dimples and a quick laugh, and her name was Dawn Borden. She was wearing a knitted coat that made her eyes look more blue than the sky. Her hair was brown—the kind of inconspicuous brown that Rusty especially envied.

This Dawn had a lot of nerve, Rusty thought resentfully. She had a lot of nerve, trotting along with them without even being asked. And all that talking and laughing. As full of bubbles as a bottle of pop, she was.

Dawn laughed up at Alan as she told him, "We just moved to Melville this semester, so I missed out on seeing you do all those wonderful things I've heard about."

14

Rusty thought she'd positively gag at the way Alan lapped it up, and the way he asked, innocent as a kitten, "What wonderful things?"

Her brother. Her favorite brother. Her brother who had been her hero—until recently. Now, instead of going to baseball practice, about all he was exercising were his ears, listening to gush and mush from girls. Girls like this one whose name should be Bubbles. Miss Bubbles, no less.

As usual when anyone strange was around, Jeri was tongue-tied. But Jeri had already spoken too much, Rusty decided. Jeri had revealed her true self. She had done it for the first time when she'd looked back at Mickey Gordon and giggled. That silly giggle! Then she'd done it again when she'd said, oh so wistfully, that those boys might still catch up with them. But though the handwriting had been on the wall plainly enough, she, Rusty Eastman, hadn't wanted to believe her own eyes and ears. She'd wanted to go on believing that Jeri was still her close friend.

Many a time since the first week of their first year in junior high they had marveled at their good fortune in finding each other among all the boy-crazy girls and the girl-chasing boys, and all the other chirps and mopes and just plain ughs. They had spurned the friendship of other girls, even though some people—parents, for instance—had tried to warn them. So now what they'd been warned against was coming to pass. Their undying friendship was about to die.

Rusty became aware that Dawn Borden was speaking to her, and also to Jeri. "I suppose you two just can't wait," Dawn was saying, "to get out of junior high and into high? I remember, I thought graduation day would never arrive."

As usual, Jeri made no attempt to answer. For the first time Rusty felt herself resenting the fact that she always had to speak for both of them. It was time Jeri learned to speak for herself, she decided crossly.

"As far as I am concerned," Rusty told Dawn loftily, "I can't say I am in any rush to get to high school." It wasn't true, of course, and she really didn't know why she'd said it. She wished she could take back her words.

She wished so more than ever when Jeri, in amazement at Rusty's untruth, exclaimed, "Why, Rusty Eastman! You've said a million times you wish you were at Carver right now!"

She felt Alan's eyes on her. And she felt her face getting all hot and red. She wanted to fall through to China and stay there forever.

To make matters worse, that horrible Dawn

Borden said sweetly, "You have the prettiest red hair, Rusty, and your wave looks so natural. Don't tell me you not only have natural red hair but a natural curl? I mean a *real* permanent wave, and not the kind that grows out?"

Nobody spoke up for her. Not Jeri, of course. Even Alan didn't come to her rescue. He was too busy smiling admiringly at Miss Bubbles.

"Yes," she was forced to admit. "Yes, and I'm stuck with it."

Dawn laughed, as if Rusty had said something very amusing. And Jeri was laughing too!

They were nearing Jeri's corner. "See you after," Jeri told Rusty. It was what they always said. After lunch. After dinner. In person or on the phone, they usually managed to get together.

Before leaving them, Jeri, her self-consciousness scarcely showing, told Dawn, "It was nice meeting you."

Rusty tried to tell herself she was pleased at her friend's show of poise. But she wasn't really. Neither was she pleased when Dawn said, "What a darling girl."

Rusty corrected the statement silently. Jeri had been a faithful friend. Now she was a traitor to the cause. She had betrayed their ideals. Jeri was just another girl now, just another silly. Rusty was glad she was almost home. She felt as if she might actually burst into tears, right out on the street in front of the whole world. She hated to cry. After she cried, her nose got all stopped up, and her eyeballs felt like two boiled onions. She wasn't going to cry. She just wasn't!

One thing helped. A car, a nice shiny sedan, stopped at the curb, and the two girls in it offered Dawn Borden a ride. All the while they smiled prettily at Alan; but when they left, Dawn went with them.

Rusty's eyes turned toward home, a two-story gray frame house about a block away. Her mother was there, for the battered blue station wagon was in the driveway. Above the garage was the "roost," her very own room. She could see the windows of her roost beyond the leafless trees. A jogging stairway led to the safety of her room. She would shut her door, maybe even lock it. Then she would be alone. At the moment she could think of nothing more desirable.

They were almost at their walk when Alan asked, "What's with you lately anyway, Rusty?"

"With *me?*" she scoffed. "You mean what's with that Miss Bubbles, don't you?"

Alan answered sharply, "I suppose you're referring to Dawn Borden? What have you got against her, for corn's sake?"

"You mean you're so dense that you didn't get it? All that bit about my hair. All those phony compliments. Just to impress you."

"She said something about it being red. And pretty. And naturally curly. And it is. So what's to squawk about?"

Squawk? First the slam book accused her of being a flapper, always flapping about something. Now Alan accused her of squawking. And Jeri had betrayed her. It was too much. "How would you like it," she demanded fiercely, "if you had carroty red hair?"

"Oh, for—" Alan managed to halt his words of impatience. "You've got a thing about your hair, Rusty. And I'm not just yakking. The funny part is, one of these days you'll find out it's not at all the way you think it is. You might even be glad you have curly red hair."

"Huh! It's easy for you to say. You haven't got red hair. Nobody else in the family has red hair." She glared down at the muddy tracks on the sidewalk leading to their front door, marks left by the twins' bikes.

Alan groaned. "Come off it, Rosalind."

Nothing was more aggravating to Rusty than to have one of her brothers call her Rosalind, and Alan knew it. She turned on him in fury.

Before she could speak, he said with a quick smile of apology, "I'm sorry, Dodie."

It had been a long time since he'd called her that. It was the name he'd had for her when he was unable to pronounce Rosalind. Somehow Dodie had been all but forgotten as somewhere along the way she had become Rusty to everyone. Probably because she had insisted she would not go to school at all if the teachers called her Rosalind, her parents had seen to it that she was Rusty even to her teachers.

Now it seemed wrong somehow for Alan to call her by her childhood name. She suspected that he had done it deliberately, knowing that she would like having him call her Dodie. But why should he think this?

Most puzzling of all was the fact that she did like it. Just for a little while it made her feel as if nothing had happened to change things between them. As if everything was all right again. When it wasn't.

Nobody Understands

WHILE RUSTY WAS PUZZLING over this, the front door opened and their mother called a greeting. "I'm glad you're home," Mrs. Eastman said. "I have to scoot to pick up the boys at school and take them to the Y. Uncle Law dropped in, and we had a snack, and I haven't had time to get at the dishes. You do them, please, Rusty."

All the unhappiness that had been roiling inside her spilled over in angry words. "Oh sure, let Rusty wash the dishes. Let Rusty do all the dirty work. Let Rusty do everything. She's a girl. That's what girls are for: to be slaves."

Mrs. Eastman was a slender woman with an air of always being in a hurry. The fine lines around her generous mouth and between her well-shaped eyebrows disappeared when she

smiled, and there were moments when she
looked surprisingly young and pretty. Just now
the lines were in evidence as she said with a
touch of impatience, "Must we go through all
that again, Rusty? Men have their work. We
have ours. There are some things in life we have
to learn to accept."

Tears blurred Rusty's eyes as she marched to
her room halfway up to the second floor. Today
she found no pleasure in her roost. She kicked
the bathroom door shut. The twins were always leaving it open. It was her bathroom, con-
nected with her room. Why did they have to
use it, even if hers was the only room with a
private bath? She'd lock them out, that's what
she'd do. And she's put a Do Not Disturb
sign on her door.

She found no pleasure, either, in the new-
ness of the maple furniture that was an ad-
vance graduation gift. She recalled her mother's
saying, "We just couldn't wait much longer.
Your old bed was about to fall apart." Her parents had laughed, as if this were a joke. But
that was why they'd bought it, of course: because they couldn't let the old one fall apart.

She dumped her schoolbooks and coat on the
new bed. The bedspread and matching drapes
were dark brown plaid. She had insisted that
she didn't want blue or pink or even green.

And she certainly didn't want ruffles. That was practically the only time in her whole life that she had gotten her own way, she thought dolefully as she pulled off the band of velvet and elastic that kept her hair from falling forward into her eyes. The hairband was her mother's idea, not hers. Her mother probably wanted her to look like Debra Damon.

She hung her coat in the closet where she had stored her favorite baseball and bat, her ice skates and roller skates, and other favorite things, to keep them as safe as possible from Alan and Gordon and Peter and Paul, all of whom had an infuriating habit of borrowing her things when they lost their own.

On the chest of drawers was a framed snapshot of Jeri, and another of Uncle Law. His name was Lawrence, and he was a lawyer; and Rusty was proud that it was she who, in her much younger days, had given him the name Uncle Law, which had stuck through the years. His picture revealed that he was not exactly the movie-star type, thank goodness. Instead it showed the twinkle in his eyes and his look of understanding.

She wished he hadn't left before she got home from school. He always told her she was his favorite niece. She wasn't really his niece at all, for he was a distant cousin of her mother's.

But somehow Rusty knew that if she were Uncle Law's niece, she would be his favorite.

He was the only one now who understood her. She'd thought Jeri understood her, just as she'd thought she understood Jeri. Now she knew that wasn't true. Even Alan was lost to her.

Maybe she could go and live with Uncle Law. He lived all alone, except for his housekeeper, Mrs. Puffen. She would be a companion to Uncle Law, Rusty decided, and Mrs. Puffen could keep house for both of them. It was the perfect solution to her problem.

This decision made her feel so much better that she took her books from the middle of the bed and piled them on the maple kneehole desk where they belonged; and then she hung up her new school skirt and blouse and stepped into a comfortable pair of blue jeans, and over the jeans she buttoned one of Alan's discarded shirts. Then she went down to wash the dishes.

There was a shortcut to the kitchen around the lower steps of the staircase, but Rusty shuffled through the living and dining rooms. Uncle Law had stretched out in the big green armchair near the fireplace. She was sure, because he always used the footstool. Her father was too tall to use it, but Uncle Law was more comfortable when he did.

There were no other signs of his having been in the living room. The slipcovers on the sofa and chairs were sometimes removed for company. But Uncle Law wasn't company. The long dining-room table was just as it had been when she'd left for school, and so were the chairs. That meant coffee had probably been served in the kitchen, from whence came a spicy fragrance that tantalized her nostrils.

The kitchen and the basement "rec" room were the two areas most used by the family. Sometimes the kitchen looked untidy, even though Mrs. Eastman was a good housekeeper. Right now the bowl and beaters from the electric mixer were soaking in the sink, along with some plates and cups and silverware. On the table in the sunny alcove there were crumbs and more dishes. Alan was there, helping himself to the fragrant coffee cake. She should have known he would be stuffing himself. Just stuffing—not doing anything helpful, of course.

Alan said, "If you want some of this, you'd better grab before it's all gone."

She snatched a big square of the sugary, cinnamon-flavored confection, still slightly warm from the oven.

Alan spoke again. "Mother said to be sure to wash the coffee pot."

After eating the cake, she felt better. Maybe she'd been on the verge of starvation. She no longer minded that Alan was lingering in the kitchen.

Rusty peered into the coffee pot. "I never know what to do with the coffee crumbs."

At that Alan let out a whoop of laughter. "Crumbs! Coffee doesn't have crumbs, you crumb. Coffee has grounds."

Even before he finished speaking she was full of anger again, and frustration and despair. She and Alan had always banded together, the two of them against the three younger ones in the family. But ever since the change in Alan, nothing seemed right any more.

"You're so smart!" she lashed out at him. "Too smart to study when you should! Too smart to say good-bye and hang up when goofy girls phone you all the time! And why weren't you out shaping up with the baseball team today?" There, she'd said it. She'd finally told him off!

When he didn't answer, she went on, "You know you could get dropped from the team if you don't keep up your grades. Just because you happen to be the son of the coach doesn't give you any special privileges, you know."

She waited for him to snap back at her. When he didn't she stole a look his way as she emptied the coffee grounds down the drain. He was sitting at the table near the big kitchen window. With the sunlight shining on him, he looked so handsome!

He spoke quietly. "Don't go broadcasting this, Rusty, but I've about decided no more Carver teams for me."

She was surprised that he didn't sound mad, and she was hurt that he should think he had to warn her not to "broadcast" what he said.

And she was filled with dismay at the mere thought of Alan not being on any more Carver High School teams! The coffee pot all but slipped through her fingers. "But—why?" she asked falteringly. "Alan, you're a star. A natural. Everyone says so."

"You wouldn't understand, Rusty," Alan said.

"Understand? What's to understand?" she shouted.

He brushed the cake crumbs from the front of his brown checked sport jacket and stood up. "When you grow up, you'll understand that there are other things to enjoy. I've had it with sports. Up to here. For more reasons than one."

She wanted to question him. She wanted to know all the reasons, whatever they were. But Alan just smiled his most charming smile and exited, leaving her with the unwashed dishes.

The Awful Truth

THERE COULD BE only one reason for this ghastly change in Alan. He'd said there were "other things to enjoy." That had to mean girls. Girls, that's who were responsible!

Alan, *Alan!* Rusty thought despairingly as she sudsed and rinsed the dishes. It wouldn't have mattered so much if it had been Gordon or Peter or Paul who'd changed. She had never been true pals with the younger boys, the way she'd been with Alan.

And now Alan had suddenly turned into a stranger. He had been a star, an all-around athlete, people had said even back when he was in seventh grade. It made her feel sick as she remembered how the stands had rocked with shouts of "Eastman! Eastman!" as Alan made one more basket, or threw a game-saving forward pass, or drove in a winning run.

And now her father was trying to get a baseball team in shape for the season's first game. Carver had never done too well in baseball. They needed Alan. And where was Alan while her father was sweating it out to put a team together? Alan was acting all googly over Miss Bubbles: that's where Alan was!

Rusty wanted to open her mouth and howl, just thinking about it. Instead, she shut herself in her room and stacked her loudest records on the player to close out her unhappy thoughts while she did her homework.

Then all of a sudden a catastrophic thought struck her. What if the real reason Alan was quitting sports was that he had a fatal affliction? Probably something that could take him in a flash. And he was being brave, trying to keep the knowledge of his tragic disease from everyone, even his parents.

That was it, she was sure. That must be it. Hadn't Alan been a most sickly child? Hadn't he almost died?

Even while her heart continued to beat wildly at the thought of Alan having a fatal affliction, she decided this just couldn't be true. Alan was the very picture of health. Besides, if it were true, her parents would be aware of it.

No, the reason for the change in Alan just had to be girls.

She didn't hear the telephone ring a few minutes later, but she knew it was probably Jeri calling her when Alan shouted up the stairs, "For you, Rusty."

She yelled back, "I'm busy."

"For you," he insisted.

With protesting groans, she left her desk and went up to the next landing where the extension phone was.

Jeri started at once to talk about Dawn Borden, only to switch in mid-sentence to discussing the thrilling tone of Alan's voice. "His voice is so deep," Jeri declared, pausing to sigh briefly, "it's hard to believe it's not a man speaking."

"Some man," Rusty snapped. She asked abruptly, "Did you have anything special to talk about? I was in the midst of a lulu of a math problem."

Though Jeri never had understood why Rusty found mathematics challenging, she was immediately sympathetic. "Call me after."

"No, I don't think so—" Rusty started to say, only to realize that Jeri had hung up.

Back in her room, Rusty could not concentrate on math or anything else. She kicked off her loafers and pawed around in her clothes closet for her good old sneakers. Spring was at hand, and she'd need her sneakers. Nothing was more comfortable—except bare feet, of course, but her mother had the peculiar notion that she was too old to go barefoot.

When at last the sneakers came to light, they were not in as good condition as Rusty had remembered. In fact, they were practically beat. She'd probably have to get a new pair and start dirtying them up.

She prowled restlessly about the room. Her roost. She'd always thought this was the best room in the whole house, even before she got new furniture. It wasn't as big as the rooms upstairs. But nobody else she knew had a room halfway between the first and second floors. Being in this room over the garage sometimes was a little like being in a tree house, especially in summer, when leafy branches of the Chinese elms swayed in the wind outside her open windows.

As she turned her attention to her homework, she heard someone calling her name again. She unlocked the door to bawl down the stairs, "What do you want?"

Either Peter or Paul answered. The sound of their voices was as identical as everything else about them. "Time to eat," the eight-year-old piped.

Time to eat. And she hadn't been called downstairs even to set the table. Something was wrong somewhere.

She hustled down to see. Besides, she was hungry. The good pot-roast-with-onions smell that had been sneaking out from the tight lid of the Dutch oven suddenly made her stomach hurt with hunger.

They were all waiting for her at the long table in the kitchen alcove. Her father was at one end of the table, his eyes as bright and his skin as glowing as Alan's. Her mother sat at the other end of the table, a crisp cotton apron protecting her trim skirt and blouse. Gordon sat between the twins; all of them looked alike, faces round and rosy, and a dimple in each chin.

Alan's place was next to hers. He stood up, and just as she reached the table, he pulled her chair back.

"Oh no, you don't!" she cried out wrathfully, trying to pull the chair from his grasp. Too late she realized that Alan was not trying to trick her and land her on the floor. Instead, he was making like a gentleman, or a waiter in a fancy restaurant.

The three boys on the other side of the table hooted with laughter. Rusty felt her face burn as if all her freckles had turned into lighted candles.

Mr. Eastman said, "Quiet, boys," and they were quiet, though still grinning.

With a smile that asked for her understanding he said, "We thought it was time we treated you like a young lady, Rusty. With all these boys cluttering up the place, sometimes it's a little hard to remember that we have a young lady in the family."

A young lady? Who wanted to be treated like a young lady? Rusty sank into her chair in consternation.

Her mother said, "And we have some good news for you, Rusty. The boys have agreed to lend a hand with some of the housework, because we want to be sure you aren't doing more than your share of the chores."

Gordon said, "Yeah, how about that, Rusty?"

Paul said, "We're even going to dust and stuff."

Peter said, "Yeah, dust and sometimes dry dishes. And other stuff."

Rusty's mouth opened wider and wider. They'd decided that the boys were to help her. But this wasn't what she'd really wanted. They should have asked her. They shouldn't have decided everything without asking her. What she'd wanted was to do the things the boys did. Burn the trash. Take out the garbage. Clear out the junk that accumulated in the garage. She wanted to do what they did. She didn't want them doing what she did.

Alan said with a snort, "We'll all have house-maid's knee." Everyone laughed then.

Rusty felt her mother's eyes on her. She didn't dare return the look. She was relieved when her father quieted everyone by asking, "Whose turn is it to say grace tonight?"

. It wasn't her turn, thank goodness, for she couldn't have trusted her voice.

When dinner was over, Gordon and the twins each wanted to be the one to clear the table. Mr. Eastman said with a broad smile, "It must be your charm, Rusty, that makes all these young men so eager to labor in your be-half."

They were making fun of her, Rusty was sure. Suddenly the pot roast and noodles and apple crisp that had tasted so good felt all squirmy inside her. She said in a quavering voice, "Then let them do it! Let them do the dishwashing too!" And she ran from the kitch-en and up to her room, where she slammed the door and threw herself on the bed.

Now she wanted to cry and couldn't. The tears did little more than dampen her eyeballs. After a while she rolled over on her back. This was not comfortable for long, and she pulled a pillow under her head while she waited for her mother to send one of the boys up to tell her to get downstairs and do the dishes. But nobody came, though she began to wish they would. Or that Jeri would phone and give her a reason for leaving her room. After talking to Jeri, she could pretend she had only left the kitchen to go to the bathroom or something.

She fell asleep, and when she awoke it was dark in the room. For a moment she was confused. Then she remembered, and was overwhelmed with shame at her actions. Thinking back to everything that had been said and done through the miserable dinner hour, she knew her parents had been trying to show consideration for her. She'd complained so much about having to do things because of being a girl. So they'd persuaded the boys they should help her. And had she shown any gratitude to anyone? No, she'd acted like a spoiled brat. She didn't know what had gotten into her. She only knew she should tell someone she was sorry.

Still a little woozy with sleep, she made her way to the door and opened it. Everything was dark, upstairs and down. Everyone had gone to bed. They'd probably decided she had gone to bed without even saying good night. It was no wonder they'd think so, the way she'd been acting.

She pulled on her pajamas, and was about to brush her teeth when she realized that she was hungry. Much too hungry to go to sleep without something to fill her stomach.

The middle shelf of the refrigerator was the place to look for leftovers. Whatever was on this shelf was okay for anyone to take. Rusty helped herself to a dish of tapioca pudding and some cold cuts for a sandwich, along with celery from the crisper.

Sitting at the table all alone, the kitchen seemed much larger, and too quiet for comfort. As she munched on the last of the celery, she thought again of her actions earlier in the evening. Again she wished she might say she was sorry.

She could write a note, and slip it under her parents' door. That, she decided, might be easier than saying it out loud. And she might chicken out if she waited until morning.

She saw one lone stubby pencil on the small built-in desk where her mother stored recipes and other things. Not a scrap of paper was in sight, though her mother had scolded just yesterday about the way pencils and pads disappeared from her desk.

Rusty went to the telephone desk in the dining room. Here there were pens, as well as paper and pencils. She chose a ball-point pen. There were some loose sheets of typewriter-size paper on the desk, and she was folding a sheet

of it in half to take with her to the kitchen
when she tripped over something.

Looking down, she saw her father's metal file,
which was usually kept in the lower drawer of
the desk. A cardboard folder was all but falling
off the top of the file, undoubtedly as the result
of her having bumped into it. She picked up
the folder to replace it. An insurance policy lay
on the file beneath it. Most likely her father had
been interrupted as he was about to put it in
the folder.

Listed on the outside of the folder were the
contents of the file. She glanced idly at the long
list of insurance policies, and marveled that
there were so many. There was insurance for
the station wagon, and all kinds of insurance on
the house and its contents. And there was life
insurance, of course.

Moving up to the top of the list, her eye
paused at an entry that had no connection with
insurance. *Adoption papers.*

That was what she read, listed on the folder.
She read and reread it several times. Her breath
seemed almost to have stopped.

In a flash of light she saw the whole situation.
What had happened was that they'd adopted
her when they'd thought Alan might die. But
he hadn't died. Not only had Alan lived, but
they'd had three more boys. Now they were

stuck with her. And because they were kind-
hearted people, they had to keep her. Besides,
think what people would say if they tried to
get rid of her. So they were stuck with her.

Until now she had never minded that the
rest of the family had their bedrooms together
upstairs, away from hers. Now she suspected
that she had been shunted aside, away from
the others. The real family was all together.
They'd probably never have adopted her if
they'd known they'd be having all those boys
with smooth dark hair. They'd never have
adopted a red-headed, freckled baby.

She couldn't believe it. Not really. It couldn't
be true.

The papers would tell. But where were they?

She tried to open the file—but it was locked.

Now she knew why the file was always locked.
Not to protect the papers in case of fire. But to
keep her from finding out that she was adopted.

What to Do?

SHE WAS STANDING in the middle of her room. Somehow she had managed to get back upstairs. She felt all goose bumps on the outside, and shaky as gelatine on the inside. There could be no mistake about what she'd seen. It had always been obvious that her parents loved the boys more than they loved her. Besides, no parents who really loved their child would give her a name like Rosalind. That was a dead giveaway.

The Eastmans weren't her parents. And the boys weren't really her brothers. This thought made her feel so cold she had to clench her teeth to keep them from chattering.

It was just as she had thought earlier: Uncle Law was her only friend. Well, she would go to him, then. He would know what to do.

But he wasn't her "uncle." Now he wasn't any relative at all. And he must have known this all along.

She wondered what Jeri would say when she found out. Recalling that she hadn't answered Jeri's phone call, and that she'd been short with Jeri earlier, she wondered unhappily if Jeri might desert her for someone else. She had certainly shown signs of it. Jeri might decide to be someone else's best friend, just when Rusty needed a faithful friend more than she ever had in her whole life.

It occurred to her that some people besides Uncle Law probably already knew that she was adopted. Maybe they felt sorry for her because she was adopted. Or maybe they criticized her. Maybe they said she hadn't appreciated a good home and living with a good family.

She tried to defend herself, but could think of no points in her defense. She tried to tell herself there must be some other explanation for the adoption papers. It was no use.

She threw herself on the bed. Sob after sob shook her from head to toe, as if this torment would never cease. Somehow she managed to muffle the sound under the bedcovers.

No Crybaby

IT WAS BREAKFASTTIME. She had to go downstairs. She had to go to school. Although she didn't want to go to school, she wanted to stay home even less. She just couldn't bear the thought of being alone in the same house with her mother. Not her mother—Mrs. Eastman, she reminded herself.

She tried to hang her head far over her cereal bowl so her red eyes wouldn't show. The family was in such a rush to get everywhere on time that nobody would have noticed her if she hadn't sniffled. Unfortunately, after she cried she always sniffled.

Mrs. Eastman said in a worried-sounding voice, "Do you have a cold, Rusty?"

41

She shook her head vigorously, and when Mrs. Eastman tried to feel her forehead, she ducked away from the table and hurried toward the hall where she'd parked her books and jacket, ready for a quick getaway.

"Rusty!" Mrs. Eastman called after her, sounding annoyed this time.

With some of the cereal that hadn't wanted to go down still in her mouth, Rusty answered thickly, "Got to meet Jeri," and ran out the door and down the street.

She was early, and Jeri wasn't in sight, of course. For Jeri was more likely to be late than early. When they first became best friends, Jeri had been inclined to ride to school, with her mother as chauffeur, if possible. Or on the school bus, or any way available. It had taken some persuading before Jeri was ready to admit that walking to school had advantages.

There was more opportunity to talk, for one thing. To this Jeri had agreed. She was not too ready to accept Rusty's contention that the exercise was also an advantage. Especially in bad weather, Jeri was opposed to exercise.

Today gray banks of clouds hid the sun, and the breeze that had been so gentle the day before had switched to damp blasts that flapped Rusty's hair about and made her knees feel creaky cold. Besides, she was all cold inside, as she'd been ever since she'd learned the awful truth.

This morning she didn't mind when Jeri started talking about Alan. She didn't have to listen. She could just let her talk. It had never occurred to her before that Jeri talked on and on. She'd thought of other girls as chirps, but it hadn't seemed possible that Jeri could be a chirp too.

It didn't really matter, she quickly assured herself. Jeri was still her best friend, and she needed a friend. Right now she needed a friend more than she'd ever thought she'd be needing anything or anyone.

All the while she was trying not to think of the reason why she needed a friend. She was trying to forget the shattering thing she'd learned about herself last night. But she couldn't forget, even if there hadn't been that big cold lump inside her that weighed her down in constant reminder. The lump must weigh more than she did, she was sure, though this defied everything she'd learned in physiology. Yet the lump was there, and it slowed her footsteps to be lugging that extra weight along.

Jeri was looking at her, smiling apologetically. "I've been doing all the talking."

"Oh, that's all right," Rusty assured Jeri magnanimously. "It was very interesting."

"Well, that's big of you, Rusty." Jeri frowned thoughtfully. "Lots of girls never say anything but nasty things about their brothers. I guess maybe I criticize my brother too sometimes. I'll have to be more like you. You're always able to see Alan's good points." She giggled before adding, "Of course, his good points are pretty obvious."

Jeri was her faithful friend. She'd never truly appreciated what a good friend Jeri was. Not truly. From now on she'd try to be a better friend to Jeri. She'd try never to get impatient with her, ever again.

A boy called a cheerful, "Hi!"

Jeri responded in her sweetest voice, "Hi, Johnny."

Often Rusty ignored boys who interrupted her conversations with Jeri. But today she felt pleased that Johnny Howe had bothered, in sprinting past them, not only to greet them but to smile. She shouted after him, "Hi, Johnny!"

He must like her a little, she thought, or he wouldn't have bothered to turn and smile.

All during the long day she welcomed every show of friendliness. She was determined that she would not think of the unwelcome knowledge about herself, but despite her intentions it returned again and again to plague her. There were panicky moments when she thought she

might not be able to hold back tears. Only the
training she'd had in proving to her brothers
—who were not really her brothers—only her
training in proving to the boys that she was one
girl who was not a crybaby saved her this
time.

It was the longest day she'd ever known.
Longer than Christmas and waiting for the time
to open presents. Longer even than the last
half of that ninth inning when Alan had been
switched from shortstop to relief pitcher with
two men on base and Carver leading by a single
run.

Late in the day she found some comfort in
the thought of Uncle Law. She would go to see
him right after school and ask him to tell her
everything. Knowing would be a help. Then
maybe she would no longer feel as if she'd suddenly awakened to find herself in a strange
country—a country much like her own, but
where everyone else was at home while she
had become a stranger. Uncle Law would know
everything she needed to know. And he would
tell her.

For the first time it occurred to her that since
the Eastmans were not her real parents, others
were. This fact was filled with tantalizing pos-
sibilities. Her parents might be part of a team
of foreign acrobats who dared not take her

back to their own country because of a feud or a vendetta, or some such fascinatingly dangerous reason. Or her parents could be royalty, fleeing from Communists, who had left her behind for her own safety. As a name for the child of royal parents, Rosalind wasn't quite so atrocious.

She leaned to the possibility that she was the daughter of American Indians, but before she'd figured out why they would leave their papoose behind she realized that no American Indian was likely to have hair the color of hers.

The voice of Miss Andrews brought her back to the classroom and the study of the English language. Miss Andrews was younger and prettier than most of her teachers, and her voice could be soft and persuasive. It could also be sharp, and now it snipped like honed shears. "Rusty Eastman, would you mind doing your daydreaming after school?"

"I'm sorry," Rusty said at once.

The class tittered, of course. She didn't care, she told herself. Wait until they found out about her. About her parents, her wonderful real parents. Then they'd all be sorry they'd laughed at her!

Disillusionment

It was important that she go see Uncle Law, she reminded herself when the dismissal bell finally rang. It was important that she know about her real parents.

But she didn't want Jeri asking questions as to why she was going to see Uncle Law. So she decided she'd better take her books home first. If she walked with Jeri to her corner, as usual, then Jeri would have no reason to ask questions. Jeri always wanted to know everything. Not all kinds of everything, of course. Jeri didn't get very excited about things in books, for instance. The things Jeri wanted to know all about were things about the people she

47

knew. And Jeri would surely want to know why
she was going to see Uncle Law. And Rusty
didn't want to talk about that, not to Jeri. At
least not just now.

So she went home. She hoped to avoid having
to face Mrs. E. That was what she'd decided to
call them, Mr. and Mrs. E. She certainly didn't
want to tell Mrs. E. where she was going. She
hoped she could dump her books and maybe
grab a handful of cookies or something on her
way to Uncle Law's office.

But Mrs. E. was right there at the door the
minute she slipped inside. "There's something
I want to talk to you about, Rusty," Mrs. E.
said.

Rusty panicked. She couldn't bear it if Mrs.
E. came out now and said she was adopted. She
had to have time to brace herself, otherwise
she'd come unzipped for sure.

"Well—I was just going to dump my books,
and—" She started up the stairs, hoping to dis-
courage Mrs. E.

But Mrs. E. was right after her. "I bought
something for you," she said in a voice sweet
enough to catch flies.

Rusty shot a glance toward the paper bag
Mrs. E. was clutching. It was a gaudily striped
bag from the Sweet Sixteen Shop where many
of the high-school girls bought their sweaters

and slips and things. Debra Damon liked to make a big noise about buying her sweaters there, as if that made her a sweater girl.

Whatever was in the striped paper bag, Rusty didn't want it. "She's trying to buy my love," she thought, her heart beating painfully.

"I've been wanting to take you for a fitting. This is something you should have had before," Mrs. E. said, with a smile as sweet as her voice.

All this sweetness was disturbing. Was it possible, Rusty wondered, that her mother really did care for her? Otherwise why would she bother to buy a present for her?

"Try it on, Rusty," her mother urged, taking a brassiere from the paper bag and holding it toward her.

Rusty stared. At a time like this—at a time like this—this was what her mother—what Mrs. E.—thought was important!

Again Mrs. E. urged, "Try it on. If it's the right size, I'll get another like it. If the size isn't right, we'll have to take you to be fitted."

Rusty burned all over with embarrassment. "I don't need it," she muttered protestingly.

Mrs. E. was firm. "Yes you do, Rusty. You're maturing, which is perfectly natural and nothing to be at all embarrassed about."

"But I don't want it!" Rusty insisted.

Mrs. E. frowned slightly. "It isn't something

that will go away, Rusty. So let's stop this nonsense and find out if it should be returned."

Rusty looked about the room for an escape hatch. There was always the bathroom. Ducking toward it, she said, "I'll try it on in a little while. I'll let you know how it is."

With a sigh Mrs. E. said, "All right, Rusty."

She was alone. Alone with her disillusion. For a little while she'd thought Mrs. E. actually cared about her. Of all things! Of all the sneaky stunts for a person to pull! She knew why, she was sure. Mrs. E. wanted her to be like Debra Damon.

If only she'd been born a boy! Boys got all the breaks. If she were a boy she'd run away from home, that's what she'd do. But as a girl, she couldn't even go see Uncle Law.

Being a girl wasn't fair. It wasn't, it wasn't, it wasn't!

To the Rescue

Rusty DIDN'T SEE how Mr. and Mrs. E. could stand the new system of having the boys help with the kitchen and other chores. Someone was always pretending it was someone else's turn, no matter what the chore was. Mr. and Mrs. E. didn't seem to mind the arguing. Instead, they laughed, as if they found it quite amusing.

The only good thing Rusty could see about it was that it took attention away from her. And she certainly didn't want anyone noticing her too much these days. It was all she could do to act as if everything were normal, as if nothing had changed, without having anyone watching her.

Then came the day when Alan announced at the dinner table what he'd already told her: that he'd given up sports. Nobody noticed her then for sure. All eyes were on Alan.

One of the twins squealed, "Gee, Alan, what are you doing that for?"

The other twin said, "Yeah, Alan, why don't you want to be a star athlete any more?"

Alan shrugged his man-sized shoulders. "I just don't enjoy it."

Ten-year-old Gordon let out a high wail of protest. "Enjoy? You crazy or something? It's like the President of the United States saying he's decided not to be President any more because he doesn't enjoy it."

Nobody laughed at Gordon's exaggerated comparison. Everyone was staring at Alan.

At last Alan said, "You don't have to act as if I committed a crime or something. After all, this is a free country, isn't it?"

It was Mr. Eastman who answered. "Yes, Alan, it is. But because so many good things are free in this country, including many opportunities, it doesn't mean we should take them for granted or toss them away carelessly." His father paused before adding earnestly, "I just hope you've given this move thorough consideration, Alan. Dropping out of sports activity or any school activity without good reason can leave a bad impression."

Alan sat up a little straighter. His dimpled chin went up a bit higher. "Well! I have a good reason, if you must know."

"Yes?" his father said.

"Yes. I need the time for studying."

There seemed to be no argument against that, even though everyone in the family was reluctant to accept Alan's decision as final.

"Maybe you could find time just for the baseball team," Peter coaxed wistfully. Peter was a rabid White Sox fan.

"Not a chance," Alan answered with finality.

When it was time to do the dinner dishes, it was Gordon's turn to help Rusty. He spoke unhappily of Alan's decision. "Boy, if I could do everything easy like Alan, I sure wouldn't be a dope and pull out the way he did."

Rusty wanted to come to Alan's defense, yet she could sympathize with Gordon. "I know. I wish I were a boy and had all his know-how."

Gordon forgot his sorrow for the moment as he grinned and said, "For a girl, you used to shoot a mean basket."

When the dishes were washed and dried and put away in the cupboards, the two of them went to the garage and got a basketball, and then they took turns shooting the ball into the hoop on the side of the garage. They were laughing, each trying to block the other's shots, when someone called, "Hey, telephone!"

"Was that for you or me?" Gordon asked. "I couldn't hear."

"Oh, it's probably Jeri," said Rusty impatiently. "I'll go." She would rather have ignored everyone and everything but Gordon and their game. She hadn't had so much fun in an age. But she started toward the front door, tossing the basketball back to Gordon. "You can use a little practice," she taunted.

The way Gordon rose to the challenge warmed her heart. "Oh, yeah?" he cried out in his biggest voice. "I can take you any day. With one hand I can take you."

She was grinning delightedly as she plunked herself at the telephone desk in the dining room. But the grin faded as a giggle was transmitted along the telephone wire in response to her impatient "Hello?"

A girl's voice, sounding young but quite confident, said, "Oh, isn't Gordon home?"

Exasperation all but choked Rusty. The call was for Gordon. A girl was calling him, and not just one. There were at least two gigglers in the background.

It wasn't the first time Gordon had been

called by a girl. Even the twins sometimes got
phone calls from junior-grade chirps and beeps.
Until today she hadn't paid much attention.
Now she was aware that this was the way it had
all started with Alan. A succession of girls had
ruined him with their giggles and gushes.

She didn't want this to happen to Gordon. He
was a good kid. Someone really ought to save
him from this horrible fate. She started to open
her mouth to say Gordon was busy.

But there he was, reaching for the receiver.
"I guess it's for me," he said, looking only
slightly abashed.

She stood in back of the telephone bench,
waiting for the conversation to come to an
end, so she could point out to Gordon some of
the facts about girls. She ached for him as he
stammered into the mouthpiece, "Well—uh—I
guess so."

"The poor kid," Rusty thought. "Why do they
want to make him all uncomfortable this way?"

After a pause, during which Rusty could hear
the high sound of a voice or voices speaking
rapidly to Gordon, he stammered once again.
"Well—uh—yeah."

Then another pause, during which Rusty was
tempted to pull the phone from Gordon and
speak her mind to those beeps who were making him so miserable.

At last he said in a rush, "Well—uh—see you in school tomorrow. Okay?" With a quick "Well, so long," Gordon ended the conversation.

Rusty could scarcely restrain herself. "Well! Of all the kooks!"

Gordon's rosy cheeks were rosier than ever. "Oh, Hedy's not so bad."

"Hedy! No wonder she phones boys, with a name like Hedy."

Gordon spoke defensively. "Well, Eloise was there. And Kay, I think. It sounded like Kay's giggle."

"Three girls and nothing better to do than call up a boy," Rusty said witheringly. "What did they want?"

Gordon stood up straighter. Suddenly he seemed taller. And older than ten going on eleven. "I don't think it's any of your business," he said, and he turned and plunged toward the front door.

Rusty bolted after him, yelling, "Well, if you want to end up like Alan— That's the way he got off the beam—"

By the time she got out the door, Gordon was nowhere in sight. She bounced the basketball in the driveway, and practiced dribbling, waiting for him to show up. When he didn't, she went slowly up to her roost and her homework.

It was her fault that Gordon had gone wherever he'd gone, she finally decided. If she hadn't blasted him about Hedy and her friends, she and Gordon might still be having fun together. The slam book had said she was a flapper. Alan had said she squawked about things. She was going to have to learn to play it cool. Not only so Gordon would be friends with her again, though she wanted that very much. She simply had to save him from the Hedys and Eloises and Kays.

She simply couldn't let him be ruined by silly girls, the way Alan had been ruined.

Tea and Mrs. Puffen

At LAST, one spring day after school, she was on her way to see Uncle Law. His office, which was part of his home, had originally been in an old residential district. But as the business district expanded, some of the old houses along Main Street had been torn down. Others had been converted, and Uncle Law's was one of these. Two rooms had been added to the front of the building, one of which was Uncle Law's private office. The other was the reception room where his secretary, Miss Ames, ruled.

Rusty never felt entirely comfortable in the presence of Miss Ames, who seemed well aware of her own intelligence, but in doubt of the intelligence of others. So she went to a door that was reached by way of a sidewalk at the side of the house.

In back of the office Mrs. Puffen, Uncle Law's housekeeper, was in charge. Rusty had long been on friendly terms with Mrs. Puffen. Her figure was comfortably old-fashioned, sort of cushioned all around, and Rusty could not imagine a better way for her to be. She always wore dark dresses, cotton in summer and wool in winter, the crisp white collar pinned at the throat with a heart-shaped brooch given to her by Mr. Puffen before he "went to his reward," as Mrs. Puffen was fond of saying.

As usual Mrs. Puffen greeted Rusty with a pleased smile. "We've missed you, dear! You haven't been to see us in a long while."

"It's almost graduation time," Rusty offered in apology, "and there seem to be more things to do all the time."

"I know, I know," Mrs. Puffen said, ushering her into the big old kitchen. "The world goes around faster every day. You do have time for tea? Cambric tea, of course."

Rusty felt much too old for cambric tea, but she didn't say so. If it pleased Mrs. Puffen to serve her a cup of hot water flavored with sugar and cream, she would drink it—and like it.

She did want to see Uncle Law and get that over with, though. "I hope Uncle Law can have tea with us?"

Mrs. Puffen was moving as if on wheels from

pantry to refrigerator to sink and to stove and back again. "Mr. Lawrence is out of town, dear. That's why I'll have to apologize for a very skimpy tea. There just doesn't seem to be any point in baking sweets when Mr. Lawrence isn't home."

Rusty wanted to leave at once. It hadn't been easy to come to see Uncle Law, not knowing what he might have to tell her. Now she felt all unzipped, knowing she'd have to go through the nervousness another time.

But she stayed, to please Mrs. Puffen. And she drank her cambric tea, and pretended to like it. Just as she also pretended to enjoy the cinnamon toast, and the plum jam on toast, and the marmalade on salted crackers.

Mrs. Puffen beamed at her. "Mr. Lawrence thinks the world of you. He couldn't think more of you if you were his very own daughter."

Rusty felt better. She beamed in return. "He's my favorite uncle."

She accepted another serving of cinnamon toast, and of plum jam on toast, and of marmalade on salted crackers before she remembered that Uncle Law really wasn't any kind of uncle to her at all.

It was a little easier to accept this fact, though, with her stomach all snug with cambric tea and toast.

The Flapper

ON THEIR WAY HOME from school these spring days, Rusty and Jeri sometimes stopped at the Carver athletic field and watched the high-school baseball team practice. Jeri usually said wistfully, "Maybe we'll see Alan."

It was as if her best friend sensed her innermost wish, Rusty marveled—that Alan would change his mind and join the baseball team again. Last year, when Alan had played, it hadn't been a good season for Carver. But Alan had kept it from being a total flop, which it was going to be this year. With Alan playing, some of last year's games had been so thrilling that nobody wanted to stay away for fear of missing a sensational victory—or near victory.

Rusty watched her father—Mr. Eastman he was to her now, she reminded herself—coaching the boys with endless patience, and she

ached with pity for him. His own son could
have helped the team if he'd wanted to. But
he didn't.

Sometimes she wondered if the reason why
she dared not sail into Alan and tell him off
the way she used to was because now she knew
that he wasn't really her brother. The only
thing wrong with that theory was that Gordon
wasn't her true brother either, yet if she was
sure he had it coming, she did sail into Gordon.
Other times she held her tongue. It wasn't easy
to hold her tongue, especially about girls tele-
phoning, but she did it.

Most important, she and Gordon shared their
sorrow about Alan. There were moments when
Rusty suspected that Gordon felt just as sad
about Alan as she did.

Then one day Gordon told her what his
phone call had been about, without her even
asking him. All of a sudden he said, "Hedy
wanted to know if I'd marry her if she doesn't
change her mind before she's old enough."

Rusty stared, not quite believing her ears.

Gordon spoke reassuringly. "Don't worry,
Rusty. Hedy's mother won't let her get married
until she's old enough."

It was a silly question to ask of a ten-year-
old, but she felt impelled to ask it. "Do you
want to marry her?"

"Oh no," he assured her. "But she said she'd help me learn to dance."

"You mean you want to learn to dance?"

"No. But everybody has to learn some time."

"Well, if that's all, I can probably help you," she offered. "I'm no pro, but I can show you how. I used to help Alan learn to lead, remember?"

Dancing was fun. And better exercise than most indoor sports. The only thing was that she didn't see what was wrong with girls dancing together. Or even boys with boys. It was unreasonable the way everyone wanted to pair off opposite sexes just to dance. She and Jeri danced together often, and Jeri always let her do the leading.

Gordon looked vastly relieved. "Hey, you're all right, Rusty. I really didn't want to have to put my arm around that old Hedy."

She went up the stairs humming a little tune and planning just how she'd teach Gordon to dance. It certainly was better that she should do it than to trust some silly girl named Hedy.

Gordon called after her, "You won't go tell everybody, will you?"

"Of course not. That's a promise."

She was good at keeping secrets, wasn't she? She had a whopper of a secret, and she hadn't told a single person. There were moments when she completely forgot about it. There were other moments when the knowledge of it hit her like a pitched ball smack against her stomach. Sometimes she cried, at night, alone in her room. But she tried not to let the tears fall for long. It was bad enough to have red hair, without having a red nose and red eyes besides.

Graduation was sneaking closer. There was no longer a good reason for being impatient to get to Carver. Certainly there would be no reason now for wanting to be there with Alan. Or with Mr. E., who was not really her father. Nothing she could do could change that.

To her surprise she began to have a strong sentimental feeling about Sandburg Junior High. So much that when the eighth-graders were asked to submit suggestions for the improvement of the school, as a kind of legacy to bequeath to the next class, she gave her composition careful consideration.

To her great delight, hers was among those chosen to be read at an assembly.

When Mr. Bigley, the school principal, started to read her suggestion to all the kids and teachers squeezed into the auditorium, she was so excited she could hardly bear it. "Destructive criticism serves no useful purpose," Mr. Bigley read from her paper. "Therefore slam books should be banned in this school from now on."

A roar went up from the assembled students. At first Rusty thought it was a roar of approval. But all too soon, even before her smile got stretched across her teeth, she realized with dismay that her suggestion was being booed.

Mr. Bigley held up a firm hand for silence. When the noise abated he read on: "Slam books are destructive, not constructive. Criticism can be helpful, but nobody is trying to be helpful when they write in a slam book. I know, because I wrote in a few myself."

This brought a laugh, and Mr. Bigley smiled and didn't seem to mind waiting for the laughter to stop before continuing: "Because nobody signs their wisecracks, this doesn't give the one slammed an opportunity for defense. This is un-American." Mr. Bigley looked up from the paper in his hand. "This contribution was from Rusty Eastman."

With all eyes her way, she felt as if she'd been pinned on an exhibit board for microscopic examination, like some kind of rare bug. She wished she'd followed Jeri's example and not written anything.

Jeri whispered, "It was great, Rusty."

She knew better. Especially after she heard a few comments from other members of the class. One boy said, "So you want to be a book banner. Don't you know that's Hitler stuff?"

Usually she would have argued the point. She
had always liked an argument. But she remembered what had been said about her in the slam
book. A flapper, always flapping about something, it said. Maybe she should have taken
that to heart before writing the composition.

She heard someone say, "She can dish it out,
but it seems she can't take it."

Maybe she couldn't. She certainly didn't take
it very well when she found out that Jeri was
invited to Debra's party and she wasn't.

She had been so sure she wouldn't mind if
she wasn't invited to any pregraduation parties.
Jeri tried not to let her know about the invitation. It all came out when someone paused
to ask Jeri, "Who's dragging you to Debra's?"

Jeri insisted afterward, "It won't be any fun,
Rusty. Not without you. Maybe I should tell
Debra I can't come."

She didn't mean it, of course. But it helped
a little to have her say it. It also helped Rusty
a little to tell herself that the reason she hadn't
been invited was because she'd written about
Debra in a slam book. It helped even though
she knew this wasn't the reason. The reason was
that no boy would want to take her.

Jeri was going to the party with Mickey Gordon. Mickey's mother would drive them, of
course, all of which was very silly. But Jeri

thought Mickey was cute. And Jeri had a new dress for the party, besides her graduation dress.

Somehow Mrs. E. must have got wind of what was happening. For the next day she looked at Rusty anxiously and said, "Maybe we should get you a party-type dress, Rusty."

"For what?" Rusty growled.

"Well, there will probably be some parties—"

Rusty interrupted. "If there are, I'm not going. Who wants to go to parties anyway?"

She hurried to her room and cried, because what she'd said wasn't true. It wasn't true that she didn't want to go to parties. Not that she thought she might have a good time at the old parties. That was ridiculous. Of course she wouldn't have a good time. She'd be miserable, all decked out in a dear-sweet-girl dress. And the kids might insist on kissing games. Who needed that?

But she didn't want to be shut out of everything. Just because she was adopted didn't mean she didn't want someone to like her. Even like her enough to ask her to a party.

She tried to think about her real parents, and how much they adored her, and how they would fuss over her when they came to claim her.

Try as she would, thinking about that did no good at all. She would just have to go to see Uncle Law as soon as possible.

Consultation with a Lawyer

SHE HAD TO KNOW. Before graduation day, she had to know. What if Mr. and Mrs. E. decided to tell her the truth about herself as a kind of graduation present?

On the day of Debra Damon's party, she went again to seek out Uncle Law and the truth.

He was in his office this time. As usual he was all smiles and gay remarks when he saw her. He got up from his desk at once and took her hand in both of his. "I'm sorry I missed you when you stopped in before, Rusty," he said in his nice warm voice. "I meant to come by to return the visit, but ever since I got back, folks seem to be conspiring to keep me at my desk." He waved his hand at the stacks of paper among the big fat books on his desk.

Rusty looked back at Uncle Law. She had always thought he had the kindest face she'd ever seen. She was momentarily surprised at how near to her own level his face was now. She couldn't quite believe that she had grown that much, yet neither could she believe that Uncle Law could be bending with age.

True, there were many lines in his thin face. But his face, as long as she could remember, had been lined. Just as his eyes always lit up at the sight of her. That was part of Uncle Law. And so was his quick way of sensing things without being told.

This time he somehow knew that she wished to speak to him alone, without danger of interruption from Miss Ames. So he asked Miss Ames, with his nicest smile, if she would mind taking some letters to the post office right away. When the door closed them in together in his office with all the piled papers and books that Mrs. Puffen had strict orders not to disturb, he leaned back in his old swivel chair and asked with mock seriousness, "I suppose you came to retain my services as a lawyer?"

That made it easier. "Yes," she said boldly, "I want you to find out who my real parents are."

He didn't pretend not to understand. He said, "So you know. I wasn't aware that Carl and Emily had told you."

"They didn't." She gulped painfully. "I saw some papers." So it was true! She *was* the one who was adopted! All along she'd known it, of course. But now it was final. Absolute. With no possibility of it's being just a dream or something she'd been imagining. To her utter disgust, she started to cry. She certainly hadn't meant to be such a silly.

Uncle Law was sympathetic. He offered her his big handkerchief, and he said he could see that this must have been a shock to her. "I'm sure you know that Carl and Emily wouldn't have wanted you to learn it that way. They've been meaning to tell you for years, Rusty. They only put it off because they wanted to be sure of not hurting you."

The flow of tears stopped only to start again. She wanted to get home. Now she knew that she'd been hoping all the while that Uncle Law would somehow offer her proof that she wasn't adopted at all, that she'd jumped to a wrong conclusion. The reason she had been so poky in coming to see Uncle Law was because she was afraid he might tell her it was true. And now he'd told her.

Uncle Law said earnestly, "They'll have to know that you know, Rusty."

"Oh please, not now!" She couldn't bear it, to go through all this again right away. "Not until after graduation," she pleaded. "Don't tell them until after graduation."

She was almost at the door before she remembered to ask again about her real parents.

He answered soberly, "This is something we just don't know, Rusty."

She didn't believe him. He was putting her off until he had a chance to speak to Mr. and Mrs. E. But he would keep his promise, she felt sure. He wouldn't tell that she knew, not until after graduation.

Uncle Law went on to say, "I'm sure you realize, Rusty, that you have just about the finest parents any girl could ask for. And they love you very much."

She ran out and down the street, and she didn't stop running until she was almost at Hazel Road. Then she slowed her steps. Her heart was pounding a crazy beat. Ahead she could see the two-story gray frame house with white shutters. The blue station wagon was in the driveway. The Eastmans were probably all at home.

Uncle Law was right about one thing. They were fine parents. But it was the boys they loved. That was natural, and she understood.

She held her head high as she marched toward the house.

Shared Secret

Much of the time these days Rusty's stomach felt as wobbly as the heels on her graduation pumps. Her heels weren't really high, compared with Debra Damon's. But she wished now she'd insisted on good old comfortable flats.

The kids had dubbed graduation "Nervous Night," and it didn't help her stomach to hear all the comments at school and the teasing at home. She couldn't seem to concentrate, and when she passed the sugar bowl to Paul when he had asked for salt, everyone blamed it on graduation.

Paul yelped, "Good thing there's no poison around here for Rusty to pass by mistake."

Mr. E. said with a smile, "Life will be safer when we get Rusty through graduation."

But it wasn't primarily the graduation ceremony she was nervous about. It was something much more personal.

Rusty was glad her grades were high, or she suspected she might have flunked those last weeks. Because she couldn't concentrate, she didn't even know why the graduating class was dismissed early, two days before graduation.

She and Jeri walked home together, with Jeri saying things like, "This may be the last time, Rusty," and "I know I'll stumble and fall flat on my face before I ever get across the platform for my diploma."

Rusty was so full of the secret she'd kept to herself all this time, she was sure she'd pop if she didn't talk to someone about it right away. "Jeri," she finally said in desperation, "there's something I've simply got to tell you."

Jeri was hurt. "Sometimes, Rusty, you really are rude. I was in the midst of a sentence."

"I'm sorry," Rusty offered in abject apology. "I'm sorry I interrupted you, Jeri. But this is important. It's about me."

Jeri did not look impressed. "Well, I was talking about me. I guess that's just as important, isn't it?"

Rusty struggled for calmness. "This," she said, "is something I haven't told anyone. Except Uncle Law. It's important, Jeri. Do you think

we could go to your house so I can tell you—
in absolute secret?"

Jeri eyed her uncertainly. "You really do look
upset. Maybe you should tell me right now so
you'll feel better."

"No," Rusty insisted. "No. I can't risk anyone listening in. That's why I can't take you to
my house."

At Jeri's there was only one brother, Tom,
and he usually ignored them. As for Jeri's
mother, Mrs. Jones always shooed them off to
the privacy of Jeri's bedroom, and that right
now was where Rusty wanted to be.

As it turned out, nobody was home when
they got to Jeri's house. Rusty did not object to
stopping off in the kitchen while Jeri piled a
tray with brownies and bananas.

Jeri's room was all blue and white. Before
now Rusty had thought of it as too frilly and
girlish. Today she was aware of all the cross-
stitches on the curtains and the bedspread.
Mrs. Jones had done all that. And Mrs. Jones
had hooked the big blue rugs. And Mr. and
Mrs. Jones together had papered the walls and
painted the woodwork. Jeri's parents loved her
very much, Rusty thought wistfully. This was
apparent, even though Mrs. Jones did shoo
Jeri's guests off to Jeri's bedroom.

Rusty sat on the floor on one of the hooked

rugs. She didn't want to muss Jeri's bedspread, because Mrs. Jones was such a fussy house-keeper. Jeri also squatted on the floor, facing her, with the tray of brownies and bananas between them. To be polite, Rusty reached for a brownie, but she knew she couldn't swallow if she bit into it.

She needed no further urging than Jeri's, "Now tell me, Rusty."

She tried to take a deep breath, but her breath seemed squeezed tight as she announced tragically, "Jeri, I'm adopted."

She put the brownie down as she told Jeri about the night when the words *Adoption papers* had jumped out at her and changed her whole life.

Jeri's eyes opened wider and wider as she listened. "You didn't dream it, Rusty? You're sure you didn't dream it?"

"Positive. Absolutely positive. Besides, Uncle Law admitted it."

Jeri's arms flapped with her excitement. "Why, Rusty, it's almost like a movie! You're the heroine of a real-life story."

Rusty hadn't thought of it that way. It made her feel better at once. It made her feel important, and she'd been feeling miserably unimportant.

Jeri wanted to hear everything over and

over, as if it were all so incredible that she had
to hear it several times in order to believe it.

Rusty suddenly found her appetite, and they
ate the brownies and the bananas. For the moment her stomach stopped feeling as if it were
riding on a roller coaster.

She was thinking of going home when Jeri
said, "This will change things with Alan."

"What things?"

"Don't you see? Alan isn't your brother."

"I know that. But Alan is Alan, all the same."

Sometimes Jeri really didn't make much
sense, Rusty decided. Walking home, she pondered Jeri's words. Was it possible that the reason she had been disturbed about Alan's attention to girls, and theirs to him, was because she
had been jealous of them? The very thought
was revolting. But having thought it, it made
her feel self-conscious with Alan, and she tried
not even to look at him that night and the
next day.

At first she thought Alan was hurt by her
avoidance of him, and this was why he announced at the dinner table that he wasn't going to the graduation exercises with the family.
Rusty had seldom seen Mr. E. look as stern as
when he demanded of Alan, "And why aren't
you going to see Rusty graduate?"

"I didn't think there would be enough tickets

for our whole mob," Alan answered easily, "so
I told Andrea Damon I'd help her baby-sit
while her parents go to see Debra graduate."

Rusty stared in disbelief. Alan was going to
Debra Damon's house. Instead of coming to her
graduation, he'd be at Debra's, with Debra's
older sister and two or three younger children.

She didn't know Andrea, Debra's sister. But
in that moment she was sure she hated her as
much as she hated Debra. She hated her for
keeping Alan from the graduation exercises.
And she hated her for being Debra's sister.
They were undoubtedly two of a kind. Two
slinky flirts with glossy black hair, and eyes
like deep pools that said, "Come here!" And
big white wolf teeth that warned, "The better
to eat you with, my dear!" But boys never
heeded the warning.

And now Alan was going to Debra's to be
gobbled up by Debra's sister. Rusty had gone
to Alan's graduation. She had taken it for
granted that he would be at hers. Maybe he'd
found out about her. Maybe that was why he
didn't want to go. Knowing that she wasn't his
sister, he probably could see no reason for sitting through all the agony.

Not having Alan there was just one more
thing to make the evening sheer torture. She

was sure she looked a fright. Mrs. E. had suggested a visit to a hair salon for the occasion. She had refused, of course. If they didn't like her the way she was, red hair and all, then they didn't really like her anyway.

Most of her classmates looked like strangers in their graduation outfits. Debra was decked out as if she were going to a ball. Beside Debra's ruffles her own shirtwaist dress looked severely plain, but she certainly wouldn't want to swap, she assured herself.

Debra, who usually had no time for her, made a point of speaking to her tonight. "Alan's at our house," she announced, "with my sister."

"I know," Rusty answered curtly. "He told me."

The first time she'd hated Debra was in sixth grade. That was the only time she had tried out for an acting part in the Melville Children's Theater. The girl in the play lived on a ranch and rode horses and did all the things Rusty wanted to do. Debra got the part, while she slaved behind the scenes.

She didn't want to talk to Debra. Or look at her either. But just because Debra's last name started with *D*, and hers with *E*, she would have to follow Debra in the walk across the stage to get her diploma. Everyone would point them out as Beauty and the Beast, she was sure.

As the class waited to file into the auditorium, the boys made grumbling sounds of discomfort, and the girls smothered giggles and exchanged whispered compliments and said again how nervous they were.

At last the line started to move. Walking to the seats reserved for the graduating class, Rusty felt as if all eyes in the auditorium were on her. Every smile said she looked a perfect fright. She flopped into her seat and wished she could crawl under it.

She was glad for the speeches. Not because she particularly liked speeches, but because they gave her a little time to steel herself for what was to come. The superintendent of schools, Mr. Martel, pointed out that this class would be going on to high school now. As if they didn't know that. Mr. Martel also said in his booming voice, "You are very grown-up now. You know this, I'm sure. But others may not have realized it yet. So it is up to you to show them. Actions speak louder than words, you know."

This struck some of the kids as funny, maybe because of Mr. Martel's booming voice, and they laughed heartily.

When it was Mr. Bigley's turn, the principal

said, "You have been a wonderful class. A wonderful class. I might even say the best graduating class Sandburg Junior High has ever had."

This brought another laugh, for almost everyone knew that Mr. Bigley said this to every graduating class.

He went on, "I know your parents are proud of you too. And I know you will continue to make them proud of you."

For just a little while Rusty had forgotten what lay ahead of her. She had even laughed a little with the others. She had forgotten, for just a little while, that the Eastmans weren't her parents. And proud? What reason had they to be proud of her?

With her heart wobbling as crazily as her heels, she made her way up onto the stage and, after her name was called, she carried her diploma safely back down the aisle, and graduation was over.

Now, any time now, Uncle Law would tell the family she knew she was adopted. And then what would happen to her?

Good Resolutions

On the sunday following graduation, the whole family went to church as usual. First Sunday school, where both Mr. and Mrs. Eastman taught classes of young people. Then the Sunday worship service at eleven o'clock. Some kids went home after Sunday school, but Mr. and Mrs. Eastman expected their children to remain for church.

Perhaps because it was graduation time, the Reverend Dr. Clark's sermon emphasized the problems of youth. Rusty liked the verses from the Bible. "Let no man despise thy youth," Dr. Clark read from I Timothy.

This caught Rusty's attention, which had been wandering as it seemed to do most of the time these days. She had been speculating on

81

just when Uncle Law would tell Mr. and Mrs. E., and when they, in turn, would talk to her about it.

She wondered just what it meant, "Let no man despise thy youth." If it meant nobody should look down on her just because she was young, she was all for that. But on the other hand she rather hoped she might be given a break because of her youth. She'd made so many mistakes. She'd acted like such a dope. All her squawking and grumbling! Maybe nobody would want her now.

Dr. Clark was reading from Romans: "The good that I would I do not: but the evil which I would not, that I do."

How true! Her intentions were good. She wanted to do right, especially now. If there was some evil trying to influence her, she'd better be on her guard. She'd better watch her thinking. Because thinking led to doing. She'd been trying not to sound off all the time. She'd even been trying to be more considerate of others. Maybe that would be taken into consideration? She hoped so.

Dr. Clark was reading from the Bible again: "Be ye therefore perfect, even as your Father which is in heaven is perfect."

He wasn't asking much, Rusty thought, appalled. Yipes! Only perfection, that was all!

But, she admitted to herself, she really could do better. Even better than she'd been doing lately. She would do better, she vowed to herself, if she were given a chance.

She prayed, more earnestly than she had ever prayed in her life, to be given that chance. During the last hymn she lifted her voice in the chorus of praise, and she had a sure feeling that all was well in God's world.

"The boys are walking home," Mrs. E. said, taking Rusty's arm as they left the church.

It was not unusual for the boys to walk home. Rusty often walked with them. But today she was wearing her graduation pumps.

"Sit up front with us, Rusty," Mr. E. said.

Even before the car doors closed, shutting her in between them, she knew this was it. This was what she'd been waiting for. Dreading.

Uncle Law apparently had wasted no time. And now Mr. E. wasted no time. No sooner had he backed the station wagon out of the church parking lot than he said, "We wanted to have a little while alone with you, Rusty. That isn't always easy to manage, with a houseful of boys."

He turned his head her way and smiled. He had a kind smile. In response, she stretched her lips across her teeth. Her cheeks felt hot and the rest of her felt all cold.

Mrs. E.'s arm had been resting on the back of the car seat. Now she put it about Rusty's shoulders as she said, "Oh, Rusty, I hope you will forgive us for not telling you long ago. We really meant to. We knew it wasn't fair to you, not to tell you that you were adopted. But somehow it seems such a difficult thing to say. And there always seemed to be reasons for putting it off. I do hope you forgive us, dear."

This way of presenting the truth—with an apology and a plea for forgiveness—was so unexpected that Rusty could find no words. There had been many times when she'd thought apologies were due her. She'd often felt abused and badly treated. But since learning that she actually was adopted she hadn't felt that way. There seemed to be other, more important things to consider.

Before she could find words to say all this, Mr. E. laid his hand on hers and said, "We've always loved you, Rusty, from the first moment we saw you. Maybe we haven't been perfect parents, but we've always loved you."

"Oh yes," Mrs. E. said fervently. "We have always wanted a large family, and it would have been the biggest disappointment in our lives not to have children."

Mr. E. chuckled a little. "With the others all boys, we've always figured we were especially lucky that we got you to round out the family."

Mrs. E. said, "But I'm afraid we let the boys make a tomboy of you. We're going to try to do something about that. From now on things will be different."

"Right," Mr. E. agreed. "We like our boys. But we want our girl too." He squeezed her hand before returning his to the steering wheel.

Mrs. E. leaned over and kissed Rusty's cheek. "Say you forgive us, dear."

"Of course," Rusty managed, and not a moment too soon, for her eyes smarted with quick tears, and her throat clogged. Hearing herself called "dear" for the second time since leaving the church parking lot was almost too much. She'd never liked such terms of endearment. Yet now this one word seemed the most precious she'd ever heard. She gulped hard and blinked her eyes and gritted her teeth, so she wouldn't burst into tears and disgrace herself entirely. It was bad enough that she'd let them talk on, taking all the blame. She'd better not cry and make everything even worse.

Mr. E. heaved a big sigh of relief. "There! Now that's over with. We haven't told the boys yet, Rusty. We thought we'd let you decide when they are to be told."

As she hesitated Mrs. E. said, "I think the quicker the better. What do you think, dear?"

Rusty nodded in agreement, and Mrs. E. hugged her hard. "I feel as if it's a holiday," Mrs. E. said happily. "We'll have to put a mark on the calendar. It's just as special today as the day when we got you for our very own, Rusty. We wanted you very much, dear. Truly we did."

This called for a question. Rusty had to ask it. Her voice was very small and timid, but she managed to ask, "And—and do you still want me?"

"Oh, Rusty! Darling!" Now both arms were about her. "We certainly do! We always have and we always will!"

She cried then, and she didn't mind so much about crying, because her mother cried too. And her father cleared his throat several times and said some things she couldn't hear because she was all snug in her mother's arms, but she somehow knew that her father was saying that he loved her too.

It was not until the boys got home that the wonder of it all began to turn to uncertainty again. She could scarcely swallow, waiting for the moment of announcement, and to hear what the boys would say.

Dessert had been served when her father called for silence. Rusty was sure she would forever after associate rhubarb pie with the announcement to the boys that she was adopted.

Her father said solemnly, "For Rusty's sake, we should have told everyone this a long time ago." Then he smiled. "For all our sakes, I'm glad it's no longer a secret that Rusty was adopted by us. She was too young at the time to have any say in the matter. But I think I can assure you that Rusty is going to continue to put up with us."

The boys all turned to stare at Rusty as if they'd never really seen her before. She wanted to duck under the Sunday tablecloth and hide her face. She felt pale and faint, and she wondered what it would be like to faint, and what the family would do if she did.

Gordon was the first to speak. "Gosh, Rusty, you mean you're really not our sister after all?"

Both parents tried to speak at once. Their father's voice, being stronger, prevailed. "Of course Rusty is your sister. And she is our daughter, your mother's and mine. She was legally adopted, and that makes her just as much a member of the family as all the rest of us." He smiled then, directly at Rusty. "Maybe more so, because we didn't have any choice with the rest."

There were snickers at that, and Rusty managed a weak smile. She saw that Alan was staring at her, solemn-eyed.

"But you'd think I'd remember," Alan marveled. "I mean, you'd think I'd remember a time before Dodie. But I don't."

"You were too young—" their father started to say.

Their mother said, "And you weren't at all well, Alan. It wasn't until after Rusty came to us that you became really healthy and normal."

Paul said, "Rusty probably brought some magic medicine with her."

Peter agreed. "Yeah, some kind of get-well-quick stuff."

Rusty scarcely heard the twins. She was remembering the conversation in the station wagon. They'd told her things were going to be different. They didn't want a tomboy. But Alan had liked her as a tomboy. Just now he had called her Dodie. His use of her childhood name assured her that at least one of the family had not disliked the kind of girl she'd been.

She smiled at him through a mist of tears. Alan would stand by her, no matter what. He was her true brother.

Who Am I?

HOME HAD SUDDENLY BECOME a most uncomfortable place to be. Not that everyone wasn't nice to her. That was the trouble. Everyone was too nice. As if she were company. As if they didn't want to let her know that they didn't feel the same about her now that they knew she wasn't really one of the family.

This gave her a most unsettled feeling, especially when she recalled that her mother wanted her to be more like a girl, and not like the boys. She wanted to please her mother. She wanted this very much. But everything seemed to add to the unsettled feeling, the feeling of being a stranger all of a sudden. A stranger even to herself.

It was summer now, and that meant the family was around most of the time—except her father, who had a summer job at a men's clothing store. Later they would all go to a lake—the same lake they'd gone to for years—and that would be no better for her because they'd be squeezed into a small cabin, all of them together, and that wouldn't help the unsettled feeling inside her a bit, she was sure.

It might help, she reasoned, if she knew about her real parents. Her natural parents, whoever they were. Not that she wanted to return to them. The Eastmans were her true parents now. They loved her. And she loved them. But it might help her settle down, especially inside herself, if she knew about her natural parents. She'd have to ask Uncle Law again.

Rusty went out into the front yard. Alan was cutting the grass at the house next door. He was the only grown boy in the block, and several families had asked him to cut their lawns either on a regular basis or while they were on vacation. The opportunity to make money had appealed to Alan, though he would have preferred being a lifeguard at the town swimming pool.

When he saw Rusty, he switched off the motor. "How about getting me a man-size glass of lemonade? Or a pitcherful would be even better."

She was glad to do this for him. Cutting grass

was a hot job on a hot day. She was proud of him for doing it.

When she returned with the aluminum pitcher tinkling with ice cubes, Alan was talking to Sammy Jones, Jeri's cousin. Sammy was delivering newspapers. Even during school time he delivered the afternoon paper. With his fair hair and skin, Sammy looked a little like Jeri. But Sammy was a brain, and Jeri certainly wasn't. Rusty felt a little guilty to admit this about Jeri even to herself.

Sammy smiled at her. Though he and Alan were in the same year in school, he was a year younger than Alan. He wasn't as tall as Alan. And, of course, not as handsome. But he was smart, she conceded. Smarter than Alan, she admitted reluctantly.

Alan was saying, "As soon as I get my license I'm going to drive the jeep. Mr. Randall offered me the job."

Mr. Randall was the owner of the news agency that Sammy and the other newspaper carriers worked for. Only one boy was allowed to drive the bright red jeep, which was used to transport boys and papers to different areas of the town.

Rusty held the pitcher toward Sammy. "Would you like a drink? I brought two glasses." One had been intended for her, but

she didn't mention that. She felt a little sorry
for Sammy because he wasn't as handsome or
as athletic as Alan, and because Mr. Randall
hadn't offered to let him drive the jeep.

Sammy accepted her offer gratefully. After
draining the glass, he thanked her again. Then
he said, "Mustn't keep the customers waiting,"
and he hopped on his bicycle and went on his
way down the street.

"Jeri said he's an honor student," Rusty remarked.

Alan looked after him with a pitying smile.
"What good is it to be an honor student if you
have to ride a bike? Boy, I can't wait to get my
license and drive that little old jeep!"

Rusty filled his glass again.

"Man," he said, "I'll sure be glad when it's
time to go to the lake. Grass cutting is for the
birds. Or for sheep. Now that's what I should
get. Some sheep to shear the grass. How'd that
be, Rusty?"

She laughed at his notions, even while she
thought again how different it would be at
the lake this year. It could rain the whole time
they were there. That had happened before.
Other years rain hadn't mattered. But now that
she was supposed to act less like a boy and
more like a girl, and now that the boys didn't
know just how to treat her, it could very well

be unbearable. Other summers she had helped
dig for worms, catch minnies and frogs, bail
out the leaky rowboats, and all the things that
came naturally at a lake. But now what would
she do? Especially if it rained?

The whole house was strewn with suitcases
and fishing tackle and rubber fins, and all the
things that somehow had to find a place in the
station wagon, when Uncle Law phoned to wish
them a happy vacation.

Rusty noticed the concerned look on her
mother's face as she replaced the receiver.

"Mrs. Puffen," she reported, "had to leave for
Ohio last night to take care of her sister. I don't
know how Lawrence will manage without her."

Rusty's father immediately offered reassurance. "Oh, he'll manage. Don't worry about it,
Emily."

"But she waits on him hand and foot."

"Then it will probably be good for him to
'batch' it for a while."

Rusty listened to her parents with mounting
excitement. This could be the answer to her
prayers, she decided. With a hasty, "Be back
in a little while," she ducked out of the room
and ran most of the way to Uncle Law's house.

He was alone, and this too seemed an answer
to prayer; for though Miss Ames did not work

evenings, people had a way of dropping in.
"Uncle Law," Rusty said with as much breath as
she could muster, "I'd like to be your housekeeper until Mrs. Puffen gets back."

He pushed a chair toward her, but she preferred to stand. She didn't dare squeeze out
any more breath by sitting down. She guessed
her breath wasn't what it used to be, now that
she was trying to act like a girl instead of playing games with the boys.

"Rusty, I'm touched," Uncle Law said, "truly
I am. But don't you worry about me. I'll manage just fine. You go on to the lake and enjoy
yourself."

"But," she blurted out, "I don't want to go to
the lake."

He found this hard to believe, and she could
understand why. Other years she had scarcely
been able to restrain her eagerness to get to
Seldon Lake and its joys. Finally Uncle Law
understood what she was trying to tell him.
He even seemed to understand how much she
missed playing ball with the twins, practicing
jump shots with Gordon, and all the rest of it.

"But don't mention about that," she insisted.
She didn't want her mother and father to think
she preferred being a tomboy. Not when they
had their hearts set on her being a proper girl.

He promised. And somehow, she didn't know

how, he persuaded her parents to let her stay with him instead of going to Seldon Lake.

Her mother said regretfully, "I wish we'd thought to get a bigger cabin this year. Then you could have invited Jeri to go along. It would be so much more fun for you with another girl. I just didn't think of it, dear. But next year will be different."

Her father asked anxiously if she was sure she knew what she'd be letting herself in for.

"Oh yes," she assured him. "I can clean the house. I've done my own room for ages. And I can cook." This would be no problem, she was sure. She knew how to make delicious brownies. And several kinds of hamburgers. And popovers. And fudge frosting. Besides, there were all those TV frozen dinners that they never had at home because it would cost too much to feed quantities of them to the boys.

Not until the family dropped her and her suitcase at Uncle Law's, on their way to the toll road and Seldon Lake, did she have a single doubt as to the choice she'd made. But as the station wagon drove away, she had a ridiculous desire to yell after them, "Wait for me! Don't leave me!"

Two quick beeps of the car horn were a last farewell as the station wagon turned the corner and was gone from her sight.

Doorstep Dodie

She hadn't realized, until after she'd burnt a few meals and served others underdone, how old-fashioned Mrs. Puffen's kitchen was. Yet Rusty dared not mention this to Uncle Law. He would surely think she was alibiing. Especially since she was finding it surprisingly difficult to get everything ready for serving at the same time. It had never occurred to her before how much teamwork went into the preparation of meals at the Eastman house. And now, Rusty decided, she knew why her mother always seemed in such a rush.

No sooner were the breakfast dishes washed than it was time to decide what to serve Uncle Law for lunch. And after lunch, what to buy and cook and serve for dinner. Choosing things she liked, or that she thought Uncle Law liked, was not enough. For one thing, she soon learned that she had to be sure the preparing of the dessert wasn't going to take so long that there wasn't time left for the rest of the meal. Even shopping took time, especially if she happened to get in a check-out line behind women whose shopping carts were piled high with purchases.

Uncle Law kept saying to her, "Take it easy, Rusty." He just didn't realize, of course, how many things had to be done every day.

By bedtime she was tired, but she had difficulty sleeping in Mrs. Puffen's bed. The mattress, which for so long had conformed to the roundness of Mrs. Puffen, sloped toward the middle, and no matter how carefully she tried not to roll into the Puffen-made trench, each night she seemed to spend most of her time struggling out of it.

Lying awake, she wondered what everyone was doing at Seldon Lake. Post cards came every day. The family reported that they had arrived safely, that the weather was perfect and everyone was having a fine time. Rusty was sure it was a matter of courtesy that prompted them to add, "We miss you."

She wrote them a long letter, in which she was careful not to let them know how much she missed them and how much she wanted to be there with them. She told them how nice

and light the popovers were that she'd made
for lunch; she didn't mention that they were
cold before they ever reached the table. She
told them how good the fresh orange frosting
was on her yellow cake, but she thought it best
not to mention that the cake itself had fallen
and that she'd phoned Jeri to come and help
her eat it up. Uncle Law had pretended that
the cake was just as good as any Mrs. Puffen
made, but she knew better. And she saw
through his pretense that hamburger with barbecue sauce on a bun was the kind of meal
any man would enjoy after a hard day in the
office. She wrote: "Uncle Law says I'm doing
just fine." That was true; it was what he'd said.

After mailing the letter, she decided to make
Meat Balls Stroganoff for dinner. This was a
recipe from home-ec class, which the teacher
had explained was simpler to make than the
kind with strips of beef. She hurried to the
store for the ground beef and stuffed olives
and mushrooms and sour cream, and for
noodles to serve with it. There were onions in
the pantry, so she didn't have to buy those.

This time she was going to be sure that
everything would be ready at the right time.
There was gelatine in the refrigerator for dessert. A tossed salad needed only to be tossed
once again and served. The meat balls were

simmering along with the mushrooms and onions, waiting for the sour cream to be added. And the noodles were ready to drop into the boiling water.

She turned with a triumphant smile at the sound of Uncle Law's voice. "It smells mighty tempting in here," he said.

Even as she told him what was on the menu, she sensed that something was wrong. Then he told her that the out-of-town client with whom he'd been engaged for several hours insisted that Uncle Law accompany him to his hotel for dinner.

When he was gone, she was glad that she had somehow managed to say, "Oh, that's okay, Uncle Law." Several times she had said it, and each time he'd said, "I'm truly sorry, honey."

So there she was, all alone with her perfect dinner. She could call up Jeri. Jeri would be glad to come over and help her eat up the mess. But she didn't want Jeri's sympathy. She didn't want anyone's sympathy. Nor did she want to eat by herself.

Tucking her lips firmly between her teeth, she turned off the gas burners and went to the back porch. Mrs. Puffen often sat in the old-fashioned wicker chairs with their brightly patterned cretonne seat cushions and headrests.

There was a little breeze stirring. Not much.

The weather was just plain hot. There had been no rain, nor was any in sight. She tried to imagine what Alan and Gordon and the twins were doing at that hour. They'd probably been called in from the lake for supper. There was a bell, a cowbell that had never been attached to a cow, that her mother used to call the kids in. Or to call her father, if he was out fishing. Sometimes she was with him in the boat when the cowbell sounded across the water. It was a lovely sound.

Tears pricked her eyeballs, and she jumped to her feet and hurried back to the kitchen. She wasn't going to cry. She wasn't! Even though her parents wanted her to be a girl, she wasn't going to cry like a girl!

After emptying the cooking utensils, she put everything away and washed the pans and mixing bowls, and she took the unused china and silver from the table and put everything back in the pantry, along with the tablecloth.

Then she went into Uncle Law's waiting room and read the evening newspaper. If this was Sammy Jones' delivery route, then he would be the one who had delivered this paper, she thought, only to decide that this was not Sammy's territory.

She looked in the sports section to see what the writers had to say about how good a chance the White Sox had to win the pennant. One thing about Uncle Law she could not understand was his lack of interest in big-league sports.

After reading the paper, she looked for something else to read. In Uncle Law's office he had books other than law books on the shelves, and she was looking at these when she decided this was the time to give his office a "feather dusting." That was what Mrs. Puffen called the quick cleaning she gave Uncle Law's private office whenever a good opportunity presented itself.

She had scarcely finished the dusting and was carefully replacing some of the books when Uncle Law returned. Again he apologized for not being at home for dinner.

"That's okay. Truly it is, Uncle Law," she assured him.

He looked at her searchingly, and smiled. "Good girl," he said approvingly. Then, quickly, "Maybe this is a good time to talk more fully about your natural parents."

Though this was what she had thought she wanted very much, now she was not so sure. There was a saying about letting well enough alone. But she had asked for it. And now he was offering to tell her.

She said, "Let's sit on the back porch. It's

cooler there." It was also darker there, so her
face wouldn't show so much.

It was quite comfortable on the porch. The
fitful breeze was stronger, and it carried with
it the sweet scent of freshly mown grass. This
reminded Rusty of the day when she had
brought Alan lemonade and had given some to
Sammy.

Uncle Law said from the gathering darkness,
"I don't suppose you'd believe me if I said you
were left on the doorstep and nobody ever was
able to find out who left you there."

She spoke indignantly. "Of course not!"

"Then," Uncle Law said lightly, "I'll have to
make up something to satisfy you."

"Make up something?"

"Yes. Because the truth is that you were left
in a basket on my front porch."

"Yours? Your porch?" she parroted in amazement.

"Yes. That was before the front of the house
was closed in."

She listened in a kind of daze as he assured
her that he had really tried to learn who had
left her there.

"As a lawyer, it seemed that I would have a
better chance of tracing the person or persons.
. . . But I was never able to find a single thread
of conclusive evidence."

She stared at him, not wanting to believe, yet convinced despite herself that he was telling the truth.

"Emily and Carl wanted you from the moment they heard about you. Sight unseen, over the telephone they made me promise to hold you for them, because they wanted you."

Sight unseen. Like a grab bag. Still, even natural parents didn't know what their newborn children were going to look like.

Uncle Law got to his feet. "Now," he said heartily, "why don't we walk to the corner for some ice cream? Fourteen flavors, isn't that what they advertise? Or is it forty?"

He didn't really expect an answer; he was only trying to make her feel better. She and Jeri had each had two of the flavors this afternoon. But she hadn't had dinner, only a few samplings as she'd prepared the special meal that never had been served.

So she agreed to go with him, and she had two hot dogs with her Heavenly Hash sundae.

She all but choked on the second hot dog as she thought of what Uncle Law had told her. "Doorstep Dodi," she thought. "That's who I am. Doorstep Dodie."

So now she knew. She really wasn't anyone of any importance. Not anyone of importance at all. She wasn't even much good at keeping house for Uncle Law.

That night she had more trouble than ever trying to keep out of the trench in the middle of Mrs. Puffen's bed. She wanted to go home. She wanted to be in her own room, in her roost, in her own bed. She wanted to be with her own family. Now she knew what it was like to be homesick. It hurt her stomach, and her heart.

When she tried saying her prayers over again, she recalled one of the verses from the Bible that the Reverend Dr. Clark had read on that fateful Sunday when her adoptive parents had told her they were sorry they hadn't told her sooner, but truly glad she was their adopted daughter.

Dr. Clark had read: "Be ye therefore perfect, even as your Father which is in heaven is perfect." To be perfect still seemed a big order. But this time she was more aware of something else —"your Father which is in heaven."

That made Him her Father, and everyone's Father. Then maybe it didn't matter so much if she never did find out who her natural parents were. Besides, she didn't want to be separated from the Eastman family ever again. Even if they did want her to act like a lady.

School Daze

THE FAMILY CAME HOME from Seldon Lake the day before Mrs. Puffen returned from Ohio to keep house for Uncle Law. Mr. and Mrs. Eastman kissed Rusty and said, "We missed you."

Gordon said, "Yeah, like you'd miss a stuck doorbell when it stops buzzing."

The boys started to laugh. Rusty laughed too, glad that Gordon, for the moment, was treating her the way he used to treat her—before he knew she was adopted.

They stopped laughing when their father began to say something, and then didn't finish. Rusty was sure he had started to say Gordon shouldn't talk that way, and then wasn't sure it was the right thing to say. All this made everyone uncomfortable, and it was her fault, Rusty was sure. If she hadn't always been such a tomboy, maybe there'd be no problem. The boys would have been treating her like a girl, and not like another boy.

Being in school was a relief. She hadn't expected high school to be quite so different, though. It wasn't only the bigness of Carver High School and all the strange faces that made her feel lost. It was the girls. Most of them seemed so sophisticated. Even more sophisticated than Debra Damon.

It wouldn't have mattered so much if she'd still had Jeri. During the summer Jeri had somehow become more confident of herself. Now Jeri was making new friends in school, while she hadn't found anyone she wanted as a close friend.

It was really rather funny that the one person who acted as if she wanted to be friends with her was Dawn Borden. But Rusty was sure she knew why Miss Bubbles was nice to her. The one Miss Bubbles was interested in was Alan, of course.

There were things she liked at the new school. Archery was one of them. It was fun, on sunny September days, to change into gym clothes and file out to the north lawn where the targets were set up. Art students used an area close by for sketching landscapes, and Rusty felt sorry for those students who had to sit so still before their easels. Action was much more to her liking.

She could scarcely wait to play basketball in the girls' gym. Then, when she did, it was disappointing, because she was evidently the only one who had so much as tossed a ball before. Miss Robbin, the gym teacher, was pleased with her, but the girls giggled as if she were some kind of freak.

That day, after school, she went looking for Jeri. She had to talk to someone. Maybe Jeri would still understand. She spied Sammy hurrying toward an exit, and she hailed him to ask, "Have you seen Jeri?"

He shook his head. "Try the east door," he suggested with a smile, hurrying on his way to pick up his newspapers.

She went to the east door, and sure enough, there was Jeri, among a group of freshman girls. Jeri greeted her with a surprised "Hi!" as if this were not Rusty's school as well as her own. "Rusty, you know Sally, don't you? And Carol? And Trish?"

It was simpler to say "Hi" than to say "No." Especially in that pushing, noisy mob near the bus stop. Evidently Jeri was about to ride the bus with her new friends, Sally and Carol and Trish, so Rusty managed to get herself pushed off in another direction.

She kept on walking, all the way to Uncle Law's office. She had to talk to someone, and Uncle Law was the most understanding someone she knew.

She was no longer quite so much in awe of Miss Ames. Before Mrs. Puffen's return she had about decided that Miss Ames was really rather nice in her own prim way. Today Miss Ames looked up from her typewriter and said, "If you go right in, there will be about fifteen minutes before the next appointment."

"Thank you," Rusty said fervently.

She didn't know what she wanted to say. Especially when she saw all the papers and law books on Uncle Law's desk, and the look of concentration on his face. But the moment he saw her the lines eased from around his eyes and mouth, and he smiled a welcome as he got to his feet and pulled her chair closer. "Rusty! Well, you are certainly a picture of the fashionable high-school miss!"

She glanced down at her new outfit. Skirt and overblouse and jacket were of sand and beige checks. "Mother picked it out."

"Your mother has good taste," he said.

She nodded in polite agreement before saying, "Miss Ames says I can only have fifteen minutes."

"Then let's get right at the problem," he said.

She sighed, though she hadn't meant to. "I've lost my best friend. I don't have a friend any more."

He didn't say, "That's what comes of limiting yourself to one friend." He said, "Jeri?" and his tone was sympathetic.

She nodded. "Jeri's changed. She not only acts different. She looks different. She uses some kind of gook to make her eyebrows darker. And she isn't so shy any more. She has new friends."

"Do you want her back?" he asked.

"I don't know," she admitted. "She really isn't the same Jeri. She's—sophisticated. All the girls are so sophisticated. I guess that's part of the problem. I'm never going to be the sophisticated type, I know."

He looked past her to a table near the door. "Hand me that book, will you, please?"

She brought it to him, puzzled, especially when she noticed the gaudy paper jacket.

"This," he said, "was left here. By whom, I don't know. If it isn't claimed soon, it will go out with the trash. That is all it is. Trash."

He swiveled his chair to a shelf and picked from it another book. The plain hard cover was darkened with age, worn with use. He held the spine toward her so she could see what was printed on it.

"Shakespeare," she noted.

"Yes. Which book do you think has the most value?"

Obviously he was trying to convince her that it was what was inside—either a book or a person—that was important. "But," she said, "a book can be attractive on the outside and still be good inside."

He beamed at her. "Good girl! Maybe you should be a lawyer, Rusty. That was good thinking. You outsmarted me. You are planning to go to college, aren't you?"

"Yes. I'd like to be a phys-ed teacher."

"Physical education. Like father, like daughter," he said, still smiling. "Your parents will have quite a job on their hands, putting all five of you through college. You could help by getting a scholarship."

She hadn't ever thought about the heavy expense of sending children to college. She would get on the Honor Roll, she determined. She could do it by getting an A in algebra and B in her other subjects.

She felt better, now that she had a definite goal in mind. It probably wouldn't matter so much that she didn't have a close friend.

She would show Jeri and the others. They would notice her when she got on the Honor Roll.

As she rose to leave, Uncle Law reached for another book. "Here," he said, "maybe you will enjoy reading this."

She read the title, *Cyrano de Bergerac*.

"You know about him, don't you?"

"Cyrano is the one with the big nose." Honesty compelled Rusty to add, "But that's all I know about him." Why, she wondered, did Uncle Law want her to read about the man with the big nose? Did he think she was as awful to look at as Cyrano?

As if to prove her suspicions correct, when she went out Miss Ames looked up and remarked, "Your outfit blends with your freckles, Rusty." Seeing her change of expression, Miss Ames hastened to add, "It's becoming, Rusty, really."

She said, "Thanks," and hurried out. "Thanks for what?" she thought despairingly. "Thanks for pretending I look nice?" Uncle Law had admired her outfit, only to add that her mother had good taste. That didn't leave much of anything to her credit. And he'd given her a book about a man with an atrocious nose. All the same, she was going to stand by her resolution to get the very best grades she posibly could.

A compliment from her math teacher, later

in the week, sent her out of the class smiling. The girl who sat across the aisle from her smiled back, and later they found themselves together in line in the cafeteria.

The girl's name was Marilyn. They found a table and sat together. Marilyn had a nice sense of humor, Rusty discovered, and she wondered why she hadn't noticed Marilyn before.

A blond girl sat down at their table. Marilyn said, "This is Rusty Eastman, Dolores."

Dolores turned to her. "Eastman?" she said.

"Yes, my father is the coach," Rusty said proudly. For the first time she felt that it didn't matter whether anyone knew she was the Eastmans' adopted daughter. Adopted or not, she was proud that her name was Eastman.

"Well!" Dolores said. "I didn't know we had another Eastman in school. Where've you been hiding, Rusty?"

Rusty snickered. "I thought freshmen were supposed to be unseen and unheard." That was not bad for an answer, she decided, as the girls laughed merrily.

They introduced her to other girls, and they saved a seat for her at their table the next day. They listened when she spoke, and they laughed at her slightest attempt at wit. They seemed to be including her in plans for future fun, and she all but forgot Jeri. Even her resolution to make the Honor Roll no longer seemed so pressing.

Then one day she was introduced to still another girl. This girl said, "Oh, Alan Eastman's sister. He really is the most. I'll have to drop in to see you, Rusty. Just tell me what time Alan is sure to be home."

The laughter of the other girls hit her like a slap in the face. Almost the worst of it was that she hadn't seen it all sooner. She'd gone along like a chirp, silly and giggly. Thinking they all liked her. When all the time they weren't really interested in her at all.

The one they were interested in was Alan.

What's in a Name?

Rusty was not only furious with herself. She was furious with Alan. She wished she could pummel him again the way she sometimes had when they were small. She even wanted him to hit back, so she could "rassle" with him until one or both of them gasped for breath. It might not solve anything, but she was sure she would feel better afterward.

She watched for him after school, but she stayed behind at a safe distance when she saw that Dawn Borden was with him. She didn't want to have to talk to Dawn. She was in no mood for bubbles. She didn't want to talk to anyone except Alan, and for him she had plenty stored up. Words boiled inside her, in a frenzy to get out.

She had to brake her steps when a car swerved to the curb ahead of her, a door swung open, and a boy's voice offered, "Drive you home, Dawn?" It was a convertible this time, and just as she had that other time, Dawn hopped in and rode away.

Now was her chance, Rusty decided belligerently as she hastened to join Alan.

He glanced her way briefly, and then looked again in the direction of the convertible that was moving so smoothly out of their sight. "Boy," he said glumly, "she sure is popular, isn't she?"

"Yes, boy," Rusty answered sharply. "And so are you."

He looked puzzled and hurt. "What's that supposed to mean?"

"What it means," she said heatedly, "is that nobody paid any attention to me until they heard my name was Eastman. It's disgusting, that's what it is."

Alan thrust his hands deeper into the slit pockets of his suede jacket. He sighed audibly. "Yeah," he said. "I know what you mean. Disgusting is the right word for it, all right."

To have Alan suddenly agree with her was so unsettling that she forgot all the other words that were waiting to be said.

He continued, "That's just how I feel about it. I tried not to. Honest I did, Rusty. But I just couldn't take it any more."

"You couldn't?" she said, not at all sure what it was he couldn't take.

"No, I couldn't. There I was, knocking myself out. And everybody figured I was getting all the breaks. Because I was the coach's son, they figured I was getting all the breaks. As if I didn't have any credit due me at all. Being on the team just wasn't worth it. Maybe when I get to college I'll go out for a team again. But not at Carver. No, sir! Not unless they get a new coach."

Her own grievance was forgotten as she stared at Alan. At last he had told her why he'd quit sports. He'd quit because his name was Eastman. Because he was the coach's son. Because nobody—or so he said—gave him any credit for what he was able to do.

But this made no sense. Not really. Even though Alan obviously thought it did. It just made no sense at all.

Help Wanted

How bad could things get? When the six-week marking period ended, Rusty learned that she hadn't made the Honor Roll. It was her grade in English that did it. A miserable C minus, when she should have had a B. If only she had stuck to the books on the list instead of tackling *Cyrano de Bergerac*.

She had been prepared to be sympathetic toward Cyrano. Hadn't she suffered all her life because of her curly red hair—not to mention her freckles? What she wasn't prepared for was all the love mush. The dueling was okay. But that dumb Roxanne. Roxanne was thickheaded not to see that even if Cyrano did have a horrible nose, he was the good guy. Rocks-in-the-head-Anne she was, no less!

Miss Lalley all too obviously hadn't appreciated her criticisms of the book. Was she supposed to pretend to like hearts breaking all over the place?

It didn't seem fair to keep running to Uncle Law with her problems. After all, he had clients who paid him for solving their problems. But she didn't know where else to go. It wasn't her report card she wanted to talk about. Apparently her parents were pleased with her marks, even if she wasn't. It was Alan she just had to talk to someone about. Now that she knew why he had given up sports, she didn't know what to do next.

Aside from the fact that it would be betraying Alan's confidence, which she wouldn't do, she didn't see that it could do any good to tell her parents. They would only be hurt, and she didn't want to hurt them. She suspected that she hurt them often enough without meaning to.

"The evil which I would not, that I do," she thought with a sigh. It was so true. Even when she made firm resolutions not to be a flapper and a squawker any more, she soon heard herself yelling at one of the boys.

"It's my bathroom," she shouted after Paul. "You'd better quit washing your dirty paws with my soap and towels." It hurt her to see grimy streaks on the pale-yellow soap and towels her mother had bought for her bathroom. But Paul only laughed, as if he enjoyed her shrieking. Just as Peter laughed when she complained at his sloppy way of letting water drip on the floor when it was his turn to help her with the dishes. And Gordon laughed when she kicked him in the shins because he'd stomped on her toes when she was trying her best to teach him to dance. They just wouldn't cooperate at all in helping her act like a young lady.

When finally she went to Uncle Law's office, he was in court. But Mrs. Puffen was delighted to see her. "Mr. Lawrence is sure to be back soon."

Almost before she had made up her mind to stay, she was drinking cambric tea and laughing at Mrs. Puffen's pretense that Rusty had all but taken her job away. "Mr. Lawrence keeps telling me how good your cooking was."

Though she couldn't honestly believe this, it made her feel better.

At the sound of Uncle Law's car in the driveway, she excused herself and ran to talk to him where they'd be alone. Standing beside the car, with his overcoat and hat on and his briefcase in his hand, he looked almost like a stranger. As she hesitated he turned and said pleasantly,

"Well, Dodie, what can we do for you today?"

He shouldn't have called her Dodie. That was what Alan called her. It was what Alan called her when he wanted to win her over to his side. Just as he smiled at all the girls to win them over.

"Don't call me that," she said sharply. "Doorstep Dodie—left in a basket—" She was sorry at once for saying it, and she saw that Uncle Law misunderstood.

He chided, "I hope you're not going to make a career of being a doorstep child, Rusty."

A career? She, make a career of being an abandoned baby? Did he really think that was the kind of girl she was? Maybe she'd given him cause, by running to him all the time with her problems.

He spoke with firm compassion. "You're much too intelligent to use the past as an excuse, as a kind of crutch or a bid for sympathy. I'm sure you will put all that in its proper place, behind you. I'm sure you'll join the family."

He didn't say, "I'm sure you've joined the family." Did that mean he had some doubts? Then perhaps her parents had doubts. But how could they not be aware of how hard she'd been trying to please them? What was the use of trying if nobody gave her any credit?

But that was what Alan believed about him-

self. And she certainly didn't think Alan was
right. So then it couldn't be right for her either.
She said miserably, "I've been trying. I guess
I'll just have to try harder." He put his arm
about her, and she was aware that he seemed
shorter than when last she'd noticed.

As if he had read her thoughts, he said,
"Soon you'll be looking down on me."

The shock of it dried her eyes. "Oh no! I'll
always look up to you—no matter how short you
are."

He laughed, and she started to protest that
this was not exactly what she'd meant to say,
and then they were both laughing. He said, as
he'd said so many times since she was a very
small girl, "You're my favorite niece." He
added, "And I don't want you to forget that
ever, Rusty."

She hadn't been able to tell him about Alan,
but she went home feeling better about herself.
There must be hope for her if Uncle Law
thought so. And next time she'd make the
Honor Roll.

As Alan's sixteenth birthday drew closer, he
talked more and more about driving the bright
red jeep for Mr. Randall. One night Rusty
learned that she wasn't the only one who was
disturbed about this.

She hadn't meant to eavesdrop. She was curled up in a big armchair in the living room when her parents returned from a PTA meeting. Ordinarily she would have been in her own room. But tonight she was practicing baby-sitting, and the proper place to practice was in the living room. She was trying to earn money now that she was aware that money, or the possible lack of it, might be a problem for her parents. She had canvassed the neighborhood and had been promised some sitting jobs "when we can't get our regular sitter."

Everyone had laughed when she'd said at the dinner table, "I'll baby-sit with the boys tonight, Mother." Later in the evening, though, the boys hadn't laughed when she insisted it was their bedtime. There had been a mad scramble, up and down and up and down the stairs, before she finally had the three of them in bed. Alan wasn't home. She couldn't have put him to bed, of course.

She was tired, but feeling quite pleased with herself as she snuggled in the big chair, determined to be alert just in case the boys needed the attention of their sitter.

She must have been dreaming about all the money she'd make, for she didn't hear the station wagon pull into the garage. But she did hear the door open that led from the garage into the kitchen, and she heard her parents' voices. Her father said, "The long and the short of it is that Ralph Randall was just trying to be nice to the boy. It was his way of giving Alan a pat on the back. Everyone was patting him on the back those days, one way or another."

Her mother said, "I know. And it spoiled him."

"Before that," her father said, "I'm afraid you and I also spoiled him, Emily."

"Yes," she sighed. "And Rusty spoiled him. And now he thinks he should be hired to drive a jeep as soon as he gets his license. Which is pretty silly."

Her father sounded tired. "Not only silly. But downright dangerous. He hasn't had enough driving practice to take on a job like that."

"And besides, he's just got to bring his grades up," Mrs. Eastman added.

Rusty crept quietly up the stairs and into bed. Apparently Alan wasn't going to be allowed to drive the jeep. It would be a blow to him. Yet her parents were right. Even if Mr. Randall were foolish enough to trust his jeep to an inexperienced driver, it would not be right to let Alan take the job. As her father had said, it could be downright dangerous.

What if he ran into someone or something? It might affect all the rest of his life.

They had spoiled him, they'd said. And she had spoiled him. She'd never thought of it that way before. Giving Alan lots of attention, putting him first in everything, had just seemed natural. But if she had helped to spoil him, then maybe it was her duty to help unspoil him.

Someone should break the news to Alan, Rusty thought, and not let him go on thinking Mr. Randall would hire him to drive the red jeep. It wasn't fair to Alan not to tell him. Even if he was spoiled—and she knew he was —someone should tell him, before everybody else knew and he didn't.

She thought of Sammy Jones. After all, Sammy worked for Mr. Randall. It would be natural for him to break the news. Rusty wondered if she could get up enough nerve to speak to him about it.

The first snowfall of the season gave her an excuse for being outside when it was time for the paper to be delivered. Though their sidewalks were already clear of snow, she pushed the shovel across the walk as she waited.

Today Sammy was playing it safe and using a shopping cart to transport his papers instead of his bike. Alan would consider a shopping cart beneath his dignity, Rusty realized with a pang, even while she admired Sammy for not being concerned about minor things such as whether someone might laugh at him for pushing a cart.

He handed her a paper with a smile and a cheerful "Hi!"

His eyes, she noted again, were not at all like Jeri's. He didn't need gook on his eyebrows and lashes to improve the appearance of his eyes. Their sparkle took care of everything. Rusty said, "I guess you wouldn't want lemonade today. But I could make you some hot chocolate."

He looked pleased. "I'd like that. But I'd probably lose my job."

"Oh." He was working in order to go to college, she remembered Jeri telling her. She wondered if she dared delay him, and then found the words spilling out. "I guess you know about Alan wanting to drive the jeep?"

He grinned. "Who doesn't?"

"Well—I guess he's not going to have the chance."

Sammy didn't look at all surprised. "That figures," he said.

"Oh! Well—I guess maybe he doesn't really deserve it. But do you suppose you could break the news to him?" Somehow she knew that she

didn't have to spell out all the reasons to
Sammy.

He looked at her intently, his eyes probing
like X rays. Then he said, "You know, you're a
very nice girl, Rusty."

Flustered, she said, "Oh, thank you, Sammy,"
and was immediately aware that she sounded
like a chirp. As chirpy as Debra Damon, she
told herself. But she really didn't mind. She
thought of Sammy's words, and was sure
she'd said the right thing to him.

She was looking after him as he made his de-
liveries along the street, and she didn't notice that Gordon had arrived home from school.
Gordon stood in front of her and snapped his
fingers close to her eyes. "What do you think
you're doing with the snow shovel? I shoveled
this noon."

She had a feeling of surprise that the shovel
was in her hands.

"And why," Gordon wanted to know, "have
you got that dopey smile on your face?"

Mentally she felt her lips and knew they
formed a smile. And they kept right on forming
a smile as she said cheerfully, "None of your
business." She tossed the shovel at Gordon and
went running into the house.

Big Beautiful Waves

AT THE MOST UNEXPECTED MOMENTS she found herself gazing into mirrors. Formerly she had avoided mirrors, and she'd despised girls who were always pulling out a compact to look at themselves. Now, whenever she recalled Sammy's words, something drove her to a mirror. Gazing into the glass, she smiled, remembering that Sammy had said, "You're a very nice girl, Rusty."

Was it possible, she wondered, that Sammy didn't mind her red hair and freckles? Sammy was so smart. She couldn't be completely hopeless, or Sammy wouldn't have said what he had. He must have meant it. He just wasn't the type to say things to girls that he didn't really mean.

What it all boiled down to was that Sammy wasn't like Alan. She couldn't help but overhear some of Alan's telephone conversations. The girls usually called him, she had to admit. But he didn't have to be so nauseatingly nice to all of them. It gagged her to listen to his sticky line.

For just a little while she had felt sorry for Alan. That was after Sammy told him that Mr. Randall wasn't really going to let him drive the jeep. At first Alan looked stunned. Then sad, and that was almost more than she could bear. After that he was angry, and he went around slamming doors and kicking chairs out of his way. She felt guilty, as if it were all her fault.

But soon he was shining up to kids who had cars. Girls as well as boys. She suspected that he talked them into letting him drive. He seldom arrived home on foot any more. She wasn't the only one who was concerned about it; her parents were worried, she knew.

The sensible thing for Alan to do would be to help the school by playing basketball. The team was going to need a boost if they were to make any showing at all. The football squad was managing surprisingly well without Alan, but the basketball team would be missing their last year's center, who had moved out of state, while another player had been hurt riding his motorcycle in the rain.

Rusty had come to the painful conclusion that Alan was just plain lazy, and that this might be his reason for not wanting to be on a team. Nonetheless, she wanted to do something to help. It was bad enough that all those sillies smiled at him and gushed over him and kept the Eastman telephone line busy. Joy-riding with any and every willing teen-age driver was something more serious. This might be a matter of someone's life or limbs.

Rusty wondered if she dared talk to Sammy again about Alan. She was sure his advice would oe good. He was so smart. And not girl-crazy like so many boys. Recalling again the way he'd said, "You know, you're a very nice girl, Rusty," she felt sure that Sammy would approve her wanting to help Alan.

If she were to talk to Sammy about Alan, she wanted to look her best. She didn't want to spoil the good impression he had of her. Search-ing her reflection in the mirror, she arrived at the firm conclusion that she must do something about her hideous mop of hair.

After thinking this decision over carefully, she broached the subject to her mother one eve-ning when they were alone together in the kitchen. Dinner dishes and pots and pans were almost all put away before she had the courage to say, "Do you think it would be all right if I spent some of my allowance to have something done to my hair?"

Her mother turned swiftly from the cupboard shelves. "Why, Rusty, I think that's a wonderful idea. Where do you plan to get an appointment?"

She hadn't thought that far ahead, but she recalled overhearing some of the girls at school mentioning a new shop in town that was up on high-school styles.

"If you'd like, I'll make the appointment for you," her mother offered. "For Saturday?"

"Good," she answered, and ducked from the room. She was touched at how pleased her mother looked. She guessed it was natural for mothers to want their daughters to look nice. Even adopted daughters.

Walking into the beauty parlor wasn't easy. She almost wished she had asked her mother to accompany her, and she suspected that her mother would have welcomed the invitation. But there she was, hesitating just inside the doorway until a young woman with a pink uniform and strawberry blond hair asked from behind a pale pink desk, "Do you have an appointment?"

Rusty spoke with a touch of defiance. "Yes, I do."

The strawberry blonde turned her over to an older woman, who also wore a pink uniform. She showed Rusty where to hang her coat, then she led her to a vacant chair in front of the mirror that stretched all along the wall. Rusty dared not glance to either side to see who was in the other chairs.

The woman ran her hand through Rusty's hair. "Would you look at this beautiful red hair!" she exclaimed. "And naturally curly!"

Someone said, "Lucky girl!"

Rusty didn't want to be impudent, but she felt she must point out, "But it's a mop! I can hardly comb it."

The woman was busy with a long pair of scissors. "It just has a tight wave. If it's set with big rollers," she assured Rusty, "it will fall into beautiful big waves. You'll see. After it's thinned a little. And shampooed."

Rusty waited impatiently for the dryer to do its work, and for the big rollers to be removed, so she could see for herself if the woman actually could produce beautiful big waves.

She watched, fascinated, as her hair was brushed and combed and pushed and coaxed and pinned and sprayed.

"So that's what smells around here," Rusty said of the spray. But she wasn't really thinking about the spray. She was looking at her hair. It was no longer a curly mop. True to the woman's words, she had beautiful big waves in her hair.

"I can't believe it," she declared, awed.

The woman smiled understandingly. "Get some big rollers, and learn to put it up yourself in between times."

When Rusty found out how much her new hairdo was costing her, she was not at all sure that she ever could afford to return. She had fifty cents left over. She was tempted to hang onto every cent, but gratitude impelled her to tip the woman who had made her hair look so different and not ugly after all. When she got her allowance, she would get some big rollers and learn to set her own hair.

The family made a big to-do over her changed appearance. Paul and Peter pretended not to recognize her. Gordon said "Wow!" as if he really meant it. He added, sniffing, "You even smell like a girl."

"It's hair spray," she explained, laughing.

Her mother said with a catch in her voice, "It's lovely, dear, just lovely."

Alan wasn't home. She wanted his opinion.

But it was Sammy's reaction she wanted most. She watched for him to bring the Saturday paper. She had a coat handy, to slip into as soon as she spied him. She didn't want anything on her head to cover or spoil her new hairdo.

When he appeared, she started at once to tell him of her need to help Alan, without even giving him a chance to mention her hair. "The thing is," she said earnestly, "I don't know what to do, Sammy. You helped me before. That's why I'm asking you again."

Sammy pointed out reasonably, "You haven't told me what the problem is."

He was wearing a loden green windbreaker with an attached hood. He wasn't using the hood, though the wind was cold and his ears were slightly pink, like his cheeks. He really was much better looking than Jeri, she thought once again.

"Alan is sponging rides. Maybe even driving other people's cars." She sighed. "I guess the truth is he's lazy, and he'd rather goof off like that and only exert himself enough to get passing grades. But it isn't fair to him. And it isn't fair to the school. And it isn't fair to my father, who needs him on the team."

At that point she wondered if Sammy was aware that she was adopted. Jeri had probably

told him. Jeri had probably told everyone. But
it didn't really matter if everyone knew. Not
any more it didn't. The family wanted her.
That was what mattered. She waited for
Sammy to answer.

"I think," he said at last, "you should let him
have the truth, Rusty. Straight out."

"I should?" she gasped. This wasn't what
she'd wanted from Sammy. She'd wanted *him*
to do whatever needed to be done.

And she'd wanted him to say something
about her hair, she thought unhappily as she
huddled on the front porch, away from the
breeze that might ruin her hairdo. Sammy was
far down the street. And, for all she knew, he
hadn't even noticed her beautiful big waves.

Straight from the Shoulder

Rusty could feel tears rising like a storm inside her, and she shut her eyes to press them back, despising herself for having ever bothered to do something about her hair. It served her right for throwing away her money on a hopeless cause.

Sammy didn't like her. If he liked her one little smidgen he would want to help her. Or he'd at least pretend he wanted to help her. But he hadn't. And if he liked her even one little bit he would certainly have noticed her hair. It only went to show that he just didn't like her at all.

From the street in front of the house came the scream of tires as brakes were too hastily applied. Someone was getting out of a car. She blinked hard, and took a deep breath in an effort to appear calm.

Alan's voice sang out, "Thanks, Tiger. See you tomorrow," and he came bounding up the walk. Just before he reached the porch, he saw Rusty standing there, and his steps faltered. Then he proceeded more slowly.

He started to speak in a manner less confident than usual. "We were just riding around —" The words halted abruptly, along with his steps. "Well, pardon me," he said in a company kind of voice. "For a minute I thought it was my sister standing there." Then, in exaggerated amazement, he exclaimed, "Rusty, it *is* you! Say, you look terrific! Out of this planet! Didn't I try to tell you your hair could be beautiful? Cinderella, that's what you are! Let's get inside, where we can gaze at you in all your glory. It's too dark out here to get the full impact."

She all but choked. Having Alan dish out all this sticky stuff to her made her feel no better than she felt when she heard him dish it out to other girls. This was what she'd wanted Sammy to say to her—only not so drippy, of course. Coming from Alan, it made her want to pummel him, and she ran into the house and up to her roost.

She threw her coat on the bed and started to throw herself on top of it, only to remember her hair. The kind woman in the pink uniform had suggested that she protect her new waves with pins and a hairnet at bedtime. Well, this wasn't bedtime, but mashing her waves against the mattress would do them no good at all. Since she'd been foolish enough to spend the money, she'd better protect her investment.

She perched on the edge of the bed, fuming over thoughts of Sammy and Alan. Sammy hadn't talked when she wanted him to. At least, he certainly hadn't said what she wanted him to say. And Alan had spouted sweet words like a fountain. Phony words.

After a while she wondered why Alan had been so idiotic as to say it was dark on the porch when it wasn't. The days were short now, but unless there was something wrong with Alan's eyes, he certainly should be able to see her hair without the aid of an electric bulb. It occurred to her that he'd had a slightly uneasy air, as if he'd been caught near a jam pot. She thought back, and recalled the shriek of tires. Had Alan been at the wheel of that car? Did he think she might have seen him? Was that why he was so gushy with compliments? Had he hoped to buy her off with words?

It wouldn't have been the first time. In their much younger days she had been quite willing to lie for Alan. She hadn't thought of it as lying then. She had wanted to save him from punishment, no matter if he had knocked over a lamp or torn his pants or smashed a new toy in anger.

Through the unhappiness of her thoughts she heard her mother's voice on the stairs, and she hastened to hang up her coat. That gave her a good excuse for having her head inside the clothes closet when her mother stepped into the room. If her eyes were red, she didn't want her mother to know.

"I just had to look at your hair again," Mrs. Eastman said. "It really does look lovely. Did Sammy like it?"

"He didn't even notice it," she blurted out before she had time to wonder how her mother knew about Sammy.

"Oh!" The word was soft with sympathy. "Boys are that way sometimes. But often they don't mention things they feel strongly. Then sometimes later, when you least expect it, they come out with it."

Rusty dared to turn her head. "Really?" She wondered how her mother knew this, and then didn't care how, glad to be convinced that what her mother said was so.

"I need a hairnet," she said, remembering. "The woman at the shop said I should wear a net to bed."

Her mother nodded understandingly. "I don't have one, but I do have a veil that will do until we can buy a net. I'll get it right now, and at bedtime I'll show you how to put it on to hold your hair in place."

Waiting for her mother to return, Rusty moved about her room happily. It was nice to have someone to talk to about girl things. There were some things boys just weren't hip to at all. In a burst of good will, she decided that she would forgive Sammy. Being a boy, he probably couldn't help it if he didn't always say the right things, smart as he was. But at least he didn't say phony things the way Alan did.

It was Alan's turn to help her with the dishes that evening. It seemed like an omen. Here was her opportunity to talk to him. To give it to him straight, as Sammy had advised. She was sure she couldn't do it. She certainly didn't want to antagonize Alan. There were so few people who liked her. She didn't have a close friend. She wasn't even sure of Sammy now. Besides, Alan disliked criticism. He just couldn't take it.

Well, she didn't like criticism very much herself. She'd always been better at dishing it out than at taking it.

She might have kept silent with Alan if she had not overheard him trying to persuade Gordon to take his place with the kitchen work. "When I get my allowance," Alan coaxed, "I'll make it right with you."

Here was just one more reason for following Sammy's advice. This was not the first time Alan had tried—and often succeeded—in getting the younger boys to do the chores he was supposed to do. "Alan Eastman," Rusty scolded, "don't you dare try to get out of your share again!"

Alan grinned. "It's woman's work. Who needs it? Not a he-man."

"But you're not a he-man," she snapped. "A he-man doesn't try to get out of work instead of exerting himself."

Alan's grin faded. "What's that supposed to mean?"

"You start clearing the dishes," she ordered, "and I'll tell you."

Alan dismissed Gordon with a shrug and a one-man-to-another quirk of his eyebrows. "Now," he said when he'd closed the kitchen door, "read from your crystal ball, Madame Oracle."

As they worked together, scraping and stacking and rinsing the plates, she forced herself to speak calmly. "I know what I'm talking about, because in a way you're doing what I was doing. It was easy to squawk. Easier to squawk than to make the effort to—" She couldn't bring herself to say, "to be the kind of person others could like." It was what she meant, but she couldn't say it.

Instead she went on, "Uncle Law asked me if I was going to make a career of being a doorstep child. Maybe you haven't noticed, but I've been trying to join the family."

Alan had stopped clearing the table. He stood with his feet apart and his hands on his hips. "Well," he said irritably, "I hope you know what you're talking about. I can't say I do."

She had failed. She might have known she couldn't do it. "I'm sorry," she apologized. "I really didn't want to be the one to say it to you. But I figured someone had to."

He glowered at her. "Had to what? I don't know what you're driving at, stupid."

"Driving?" She snatched at the word. "Yes, that's part of it. You were driving Tiger's car —you know you're not supposed to before you pass your driver's test."

Seeing the change in his expression, she knew she'd hit the truth.

"Tiger? Who's Tiger?" he demanded, pretending innocence.

Now she refused to be daunted. "The name isn't important. What's important is that you've been doing things you know you aren't supposed to be doing. And what you should be doing you don't do."

"Such as?" His frown was forbidding.

"Such as going back on the team. At least one team. And studying."

"I told you why—"

She interrupted. "You told me. But it isn't the real reason. The real reason is that you want to do everything the easy way. It's easier for you to make people like you by smiling and saying nice things than to sweat with the football squad. It's easier for you to think up alibis than to—"

Alan pulled a dish towel from the rack and threw it in her direction. Then he headed toward the door.

"You come back here," she ordered in her loudest voice. He didn't stop until she added, "Or I'll tell Dad about Tiger."

By the manner in which he slowed, turned, and then smiled, she could all but see his thoughts changing. Like gears going into neu-

tral, then reverse, then in position to go forward
again. "Look, Dodie—" he said in a voice full
of sweetness.

She snapped, "Your soft soap won't work on
me, Alan."

He blinked, then looked at her more closely.

"All right," he said, "if you don't want to be
friends. But just the same the fact is that
you've misjudged me. All right, maybe I was
wrong to want credit for what I did. Maybe I
was wrong to let all that stuff bug me about
getting the breaks because my name is Eastman."

"You were," Rusty agreed. "What's more, if
you want to go to college, an athletic scholarship would be a big help in getting you there.
College costs money, you know."

Alan put his hands to his ears. "Spare me the
lecture. Besides, I'm no brain, and I need time
for studying. Sports take time, you know."

She waited until his hands were down again
before pointing out, "But you don't use your
spare time for studying. You just use it for joy-
riding. How's that going to help you get into
college?"

When he didn't answer she said, "When you
do hit the books, your study habits are bad.
Mother even says so. I could probably help you
with that."

He hooted. "A freshman? What could you do?"

She reminded him that she was learning to type on Uncle Law's old typewriter, which he had given her along with an instruction book and a metal stand. "I'll be glad to type some of your themes and stuff. And you can study at my desk, where it's quieter." Quieter, and farther from the phone, she thought with satisfaction. "But you really must try to write more legibly," she insisted. "Your handwriting is atrocious."

"Well, thanks for nothing," Alan said angrily. "If you've finished your spiel on how to win friends and influence people, let's get at the KP job. I'm expecting a couple of phone calls."

Further words were useless, Rusty was sure. She had tried to do as Sammy suggested. She had tried to talk straight from the shoulder. Maybe it would be better not to tell Sammy about it. She didn't want him to think of her as a failure.

Alan was silent until his part of the kitchen clean-up was completed. Then he stalked toward the door, spitting angry words over his shoulder. "You know what? I wish they'd left you on someone else's doorstep, that's what I wish."

Holiday Hop

S HE TRIED NOT TO THINK of what Alan had said to her. When she couldn't shut it out of her thoughts, she tried to tell herself that he hadn't meant what he'd said. He'd been upset. Naturally he'd been upset. She'd known all along that Alan couldn't take criticism. He wasn't used to criticism. She'd hurt him. So he'd hit back. It was as simple as all that.

At first she waited for him to say he was sorry. Alan could usually toss off an "I'm sorry" more easily than other people said "Hello." Apparently this time he wasn't going to say it.

She was glad Sammy didn't ask how she'd made out in talking straight from the shoulder with Alan. Thinking about it was painful enough, without discussing it.

Even making the Honor Roll at last didn't seem quite as much of an accomplishment as she'd once thought it would be. After all, what else was there for her to do these days but study? Study and baby-sit.

Her first baby-sitting jobs had been after school, keeping an eye on Timmy and Betsy McGurn while their mother went to the dentist's. They lived down the street, and she'd known them most of their lives. She got along fine in the daytime. It was when the McGurns asked her to stay in the evening that she ran into problems. Timmy and Betsy kept popping out of their beds, expecting her to play games with them just as she did during the day. This interrupted her studying, and she hadn't been at all certain that she'd make the Honor Roll.

It was pleasant to have girls like Dawn Borden offer congratulations. She was beginning to wonder if perhaps she had been wrong about Dawn. For Dawn was bubbly to everyone. Alan had once spoken wonderingly of Dawn's popularity, as if he too found it hard to believe that Dawn was the same to everyone. He hadn't seemed happy about that. Obviously he wanted Dawn to be a little nicer to him than to everyone else.

Through Dawn, Rusty learned that Alan had

wanted to escort Dawn to the school's annual Holiday Hop. "I was sorry to have to say no to him," Dawn confided to Rusty as they ate lunch together one day. "But someone else asked me first."

Rusty thought enviously that it must be nice to be so popular. Even with her new hairdo she didn't expect to be asked to the Holiday Hop. Anyone in school could go, of course. It was that kind of party, with games as well as dancing. But most of the girls wanted to be asked by a boy.

When she was asked, and by the one person with whom she wanted to go, it was almost more than Rusty could believe.

"If you'll go with me," Sammy paused long enough in the hall to say to her, "I'd like to go to the Holiday Hop."

She couldn't imagine a more thrilling way of being asked. It was as if he were saying that he wouldn't go at all, without her. "I'd love to go with you," she assured him.

He smiled, a relieved smile, as if he'd actually had doubts as to whether she might accept his invitation. But how could he have doubted? She just didn't understand it.

She hurried home to tell her mother she'd be needing a new dress.

Mrs. Eastman looked pleased. "I'm glad you

decided to go to the Christmas party. Who else is going?"

"The whole school, I guess. Or practically," she amended, realizing that there were others like herself who usually stayed away from school parties. She felt sorry for them.

"I meant are you going with Jeri? Or Alan?"

"Oh, Mother! Of course I'm not going with my own brother! I'm going with Sammy. He asked me to go with him."

The expression on her mother's face brought laughter to Rusty's lips. Everyone would be surprised, of course. She'd been surprised herself. Wonderfully surprised!

"But," her mother said, "won't you two be going with others? Other girls and boys?"

Rusty's smile faded. She didn't understand her mother sometimes. Once she'd wanted her to look feminine, like Debra Damon. Now she didn't want her to go to the party with Sammy. "We know our way to the school gym," Rusty said crossly. "We don't need chaperones."

When her mother didn't answer at once, Rusty pointed out, "Alan goes to all the parties. Nobody tells Alan who to go with. I don't see why I should be treated so—so—ignominiously!"

Everything was spoiled. She'd been so happy. Now everything was spoiled. She ran up the stairs to her room, with Mrs. Eastman following. She wanted to slam the door and put up her Do Not Disturb sign, but she dared not, with her mother close at her heels.

"Now listen to me, Rusty," Mrs. Eastman said firmly, seating herself in the maple rocker. "Alan is a boy."

As if she hadn't known that!

"That makes a difference," her mother said.

"Well, Sammy's a boy," Rusty pointed out, "And he asked me to go with him."

"Yes. I'm sure he's a nice boy," Mrs. Eastman stated. "But no matter how nice he is, your father and I are not in favor of boys and girls pairing off at your age. That's why—"

Rusty interrupted to wail, "But, Moth-er! I'm fourteen. And Sammy asked me! You mean you won't let me go?"

"That isn't what I mean at all. I want you to go. I'm glad you were invited. It's just that we, your father and I, would prefer to have you go with a group. Couldn't you go with one or two other couples?"

Rusty was almost in tears. "But what other couples?"

"Well—Jeri? She's Sammy's cousin."

"Jeri is going with an older boy. He has a car. I don't think he'd want to pick me up."

Mrs. Eastman was quick to agree. "That's another thing. Your father and I don't want you
riding around with drivers we don't know, or
inexperienced drivers. Especially at night."

That let Alan out, she thought with relief.
Alan had his license now. The family had cele-
brated his sixteenth birthday just as they cele-
brated the birthday of each member of the family. Uncle Law was present. There was a big
cake with candles, and ice cream. Alan kept
talking about his own set of keys for the family
station wagon. But Alan was given no keys, and
he was seldom allowed to drive. Rusty suspected that this was a form of punishment,
though for what Alan was being punished she
wasn't sure. But it would have been humiliating
to Sammy, who was a junior even if he was still
fifteen, to be told that her brother would drive
them.

"Sammy would prefer to walk," she stated
firmly. There hadn't been time for them to decide about details, but she felt certain that
Sammy would agree with her on this.

Mrs. Eastman brightened a little. "I'm glad,"
she said. "In fact, now that we've talked it
over, I'm inclined to think it might be all right
for you and Sammy to go alone. The two of you.
I'll see what your father thinks about it."

She rose to return downstairs. "When you're a

mother, you'll understand that parents feel a special concern for daughters." She turned back to say with a smile, "I'm sure you will have a wonderful time. And we'll go shopping for a dress after school Friday. Everything will work out just fine. You'll have a lovely time at the party."

Rusty wanted to run after her mother and give her a big hug. Yes, everything would work out all right now, and she'd have a lovely time at the party. All because she was a girl. Once she'd thought she wanted to be a boy. Being a girl was better. Being a girl was special. Wasn't that what her mother was trying to tell her?

Deciding on the right thing to wear to the party was agonizing, yet thrilling too. It was fun discussing this with Dawn and other girls who gathered around her, and accepted Rusty because she was with Dawn. Some of the girls said they'd probably wear pastel sweaters with matching skirts. Somehow Rusty felt it wouldn't be right to wear something so much like what she wore to school every day. She wanted Sammy to know that she appreciated being asked to the Hop by an upperclassman, and what she wore was one way of letting him know.

She almost passed by a two-piece beige dress on the rack she was pawing through rather frantically. Fortunately she remembered that

Miss Ames had said her beige and sand outfit
was becoming. So she tried the dress on. Even
before the clerk said, "That looks nice on you,"
and her mother said, "Yes, it really does," she
knew this was her dress for the Holiday Hop.
It was a dress-up dress, but not a partyish
dress.

By now she had learned to put up her hair so
that most days it looked presentable. Other days
she rebelled against "all the monkey business."
With the holiday party coming up, she welcomed her mother's suggestion that she make
another trip to the beauty salon.

"For one thing," her mother said, "your hair
needs thinning again."

She really didn't mind that several of the
pink-uniformed hairdressers teased her about
her date. "Your beau will have the prettiest girl
there," one hairdresser insisted.

Nobody had ever said before that she was
pretty. Saying it didn't make it true, of course,
but it gave her a nice warm feeling inside. She
wanted to tell them about Sammy, and how
wonderful he was, but she didn't want them to
laugh at anything she might say about him. If
they teased her, that didn't much matter. In
fact, she was finding it rather pleasant to be
teased about a boy. But she didn't want them
making fun of Sammy.

On the night of the party, she was ready early and waiting for Sammy. Her father waited with her. "You understand," he cautioned, "that you are to come directly home when the party is over?"

Rusty assured him that she understood.

To her acute embarrassment, her father repeated his words to Sammy.

Sammy answered politely, "Yes, sir. Don't you worry, sir."

To make matters worse, Alan stepped past them and out of the house with a casual "See you later, kids."

It seemed forever before she and Sammy were finally allowed to leave for the party. Sammy would never ask her anywhere ever again, she was sure.

Show-off

Alan went stag to the dance. There were plenty of other boys who went stag. There were also girls who went without boys; Rusty was glad she was not one of them.

Another thing she was glad about was that she had improved her dancing by helping Gordon learn to dance. Gordon had insisted that she let him do the leading, which was fortunate now that she was dancing with Sammy. And the combo that furnished the music had a good beat, which made dancing that much easier.

Some of Sammy's friends apparently noticed that she was a good dancer, for they offered to trade partners. Other boys spoke to her. She was surprised at how easy it was to talk to boys with Sammy at her side.

All this was so thrilling that it was quite a while before she really saw the decorations that had transformed the boys' gym into a winter wonderland. Everything sparkled like moonlit snow.

When it was time for refreshments, she was both hungry and thirsty. Sammy found a quiet spot behind Santa Claus and his sleigh, and he pulled an extra chair around in front of them to serve as a table. When the pangs of hunger were lessened, they talked. She was finding it easier all the time to talk to Sammy.

"I thought for a while that I wanted to be a phys-ed teacher," Rusty confided. "But now I think I'd rather teach math."

Sammy agreed that math was important these days, and he said it would be a challenge to teach math, and his look was admiring.

All during the party she had tried to ignore Alan. He seemed to be having a good time, dancing with one girl after another. Yet as the evening went along, she had an uneasy feeling that something was not quite right.

When Sammy went to refill her punch cup she knew what it was that was wrong with Alan tonight. She heard a boy say, "That show-off," and she looked to see the show-off. It was Alan, strutting in front of a group of giggling girls.

Another boy said, "Who cares? He's a has-been. A has-been at sixteen. That's our big hero."

"Ex-hero, you mean."

"Yeah. Ex-Mr. Big."

Rusty felt herself redden with embarrassment and humiliation. That anyone should speak this way of Alan was hard to believe. Once upon a time she would have used her fists on anyone who spoke slightingly of Alan. Now she had to admit those boys were right. Alan had it coming.

She managed somehow to keep Sammy from seeing that she was upset. She wasn't going to spoil his evening. Not for Alan or anybody.

It was a relief to get out into the crisp darkness of the night, where she didn't have to force her face to look happy. For the first time it occurred to her that Alan was really not as sure of himself as he pretended to be. He liked Dawn. That was plain. Yet he did all the wrong things in trying to impress her. It seemed strange to Rusty that boys didn't understand simple facts about girls. But then there were many things about being a girl that she was just learning herself.

Someone was going to have to help Alan see the light. She'd gone to Uncle Law too many times. She'd also consulted Sammy. This time she'd better see what she could do on her own. Even though Alan had said he didn't want her help.

With this decision made, she turned her full attention to Sammy. They were almost at her house, she realized in dismay. The evening was nearly over.

Sammy said, "Rusty isn't the right name for you. It doesn't do you justice."

This pleased her so much that she admitted, "My real name is Rosalind."

She was even more pleased when Sammy insisted, "Rosalind suits you. It's a pretty name."

This was such a deliciously pleasant pronouncement that she wanted to dwell on it longer. "Do you like it better than Roxanne?" She started to explain that Roxanne was the name of the girl beloved of Cyrano de Bergerac.

"Oh, have you read *Cyrano?*" Sammy asked eagerly. "It's really great, isn't it? Poor Cyrano and his nose. But why couldn't he see that what he had to offer—big nose and all—might have been better for Roxanne than the guy she thought she wanted?"

She would have to read it again, Rusty decided. If Sammy thought so highly of it, she would have to read it again. "I just didn't—" She stopped herself just in time from admitting that she hadn't liked "all that love stuff." She didn't want Sammy to think she had anything against love.

He said, "I guess I'd better let you go in. I

wouldn't want your father to get a bad impression of me."

Rusty was glad he wanted to keep on the good side of her father. This was undoubtedly his way of saying he wanted another date.

If so, Sammy was in no hurry. Christmas Eve and Christmas Day were happily like all the others she'd known. It was hard to find fault with anyone or anything on Christmas. But on the days that followed she could see no reason why Sammy should be in such a hurry to leave their paper. Even if the temperature was sub-zero, he could have slowed down long enough to talk a little, she told herself crossly.

Until now she hadn't really noticed how easily her parents talked to each other, and how often they laughed. That was the way it should be, she thought wistfully.

One night she heard her parents discussing a story in the paper about a well-known college coach losing his job. "It just isn't right," her mother said, "that a coach should pay with his job for not having a winning team."

"Maybe not," her father agreed cheerfully, "but it's one of the facts of life where coaches are concerned."

Rusty thought about this. None of the Carver teams had been doing especially well. But her father didn't seem worried. It probably was only college coaches who got fired, not high-school coaches. And besides, her father was also a physical-education teacher.

But what if the school should consider firing him? If he was in danger of losing his job, then surely Alan would go back on the team? Not only to save the school's record, but his father's job.

Alan needed a jolt, she thought to herself defensively as she went looking for him. It wouldn't hurt him to think their father's job was in danger. Let him worry a little. It wouldn't hurt him.

Alan was alone in the rec room. When she saw what he was doing she almost weakened, for he was leaning over the Ping-pong table, pasting clippings into the scrapbook she had given him for Christmas. He smiled at her as he said, "That was a good idea you had, Rusty. Now I can show Dawn my clippings. Remember, she said she was sorry she hadn't seen me do my stuff?"

All this time he'd remembered! He must really like Dawn. Rusty told him, "I saw her at the post office today. I asked her to come home with me, but she was busy."

"She's always busy," Alan growled.

Rusty picked up the paste brush and started to help him fasten between hard covers the

local newspaper's accounts of his days of athletic glory. "Maybe," she ventured, "Dawn
wouldn't always be too busy if you'd ask her
sooner. She told me she was sorry she had to
turn you down for the Holiday Hop, but she'd
already told Tom she'd go with him."

He looked at her searchingly. "No fooling?"

"No fooling," she assured him.

He was quiet for a while. Then he uttered
a pleased "Hmmm!" and he smiled broadly.
"You just could be right. I'll have to call her
up."

Her momentary bliss at seeing Alan look so
happy was shattered by the possibility that he
might walk out before she could tell him what
she was determined to tell him. It would be
just like him to leave the clipping and pasting
and cleaning up for her to do, while he sweet-
talked on the phone.

"Not now—" she started to say.

Alan immediately said, "No, first I should
thank you, shouldn't I? And I should apologize.
I should have done that long ago."

This disturbed her even more. "For what?"
she muttered, knowing full well what he meant.

"For saying I wished you weren't part of our
family. I didn't mean it, Dodie," he entreated.
"I hope you know I didn't mean it."

She wasn't sure. She wasn't at all sure. Alan

could be so convincing. He probably even convinced himself at times. But whether he meant
it or not—or even perhaps more so if he didn't
mean it—she had to go ahead with what she'd
planned to say to him. It was for the good of
the family. Uncle Law had said she should join
the family.

"That's all right," she said, trying mightily to
strengthen her words. "That's all right, Alan.
But there's something I think I should tell you.
I overheard Mother and Dad talking. About
coaches who lose their jobs when their teams
don't win. They talked about Dad losing his
job."

Alan looked surprised, and then he looked
angry. "They wouldn't! They couldn't! They
certainly can see that it isn't Dad's fault the
team is so lousy!" He had more to say, and
Rusty's hopes rose with every word.

Then he was quiet. There was a faraway look
on his handsome face. It was a look she had
seen many times when, as a child, he was plot-
ting something. "We'll have to fix that," Alan
said finally.

She sighed happily. Alan was going to fix it.
That could only mean he'd decided to get back
on the team. There wasn't any other way to fix
things. Or no other way that she could think of.

Who Needs Girls?

On THE SATURDAY MORNING before the end of their holiday vacation, Alan came to Rusty's room with an armload of schoolbooks. "All right," he challenged. "You said you'd help. So help."

This brought forth a squeal of pleasure from Rusty. She even squeezed his arm.

"Now," Alan scoffed, "you're acting like a girl. Aren't you the one who used to turn up your nose at chirps?"

She didn't mind his teasing. This move on his part must mean that he was really going to try to get good grades. It must mean that he was going to try to get back on a team. She said happily, "Being a girl isn't so bad."

His answer surprised her. "Who needs girls?" he growled with a dismissing shrug of disdain.

This must mean that he hadn't had any luck getting a date with Dawn Borden. She must think of something to say to help him with Dawn. But how could she get him to see that his line was phony? Dawn wasn't the kind of girl who went for all that syrupy stuff. Even though Dawn was bubbly, that was her natural way. If Alan would only be natural with Dawn, he was sure to do all right.

No sooner had she and Alan settled down at her desk than Gordon came charging up the stairs, looking for Alan. "Hey!" Gordon yelled wrathfully. "We're supposed to be shoveling the driveway, remember?"

Alan said, "I can't now. Rusty's helping me with my homework. You don't want me to flunk, do you?"

Gordon grumbled, and then went looking for the twins to help him.

Soon Peter came up the stairs to wash his hands in Rusty's bathroom. "I have to wash them in warm water to warm them up before I go out," Peter insisted. "Otherwise they'll be too cold for snow shoveling."

When Peter left, Rusty put up the Do Not Disturb sign and shut the door.

Alan didn't stay as long as she'd hoped, but he promised, "This afternoon we'll tackle it again. Right now I have to see some of the guys. It's important, Rusty, no fooling."

After lunch he went again to "see some of the guys," but true to his promise, he returned to her desk and his homework. It wasn't going to be easy to help Alan, but Rusty had a feeling of confidence that it could be done. Probably more than anyone else, she could help because she was sure she understood him.

With her encouragement, Alan finished his English assignment and tackled American history. Rusty's eye had been straying to the clock on the desk, and she got to her feet as she said, "I'll see if the paper is here yet."

"You mean Sammy," Alan snorted.

She was sure he was only pretending to disapprove, and she merely smiled.

She paused when Alan said, "You know, I used to be jealous of you."

"Jealous?" she repeated, puzzled. "Of me?"

"Sure, you."

"But why?"

"You were always the family favorite."

This, she was sure, was so far from the truth that she could only stare and sputter. "But—but —it's just—not so!" Alan had always been the favored one. Hadn't he known? Was it possible that he hadn't known? Even their parents had said they'd spoiled him.

"It finally dawned on me," Alan said, tilting back in her desk chair, "that it was because you were a girl. You were the chosen one."

"Chosen? No, that's not true," she corrected quickly. "Uncle Law told me they would have taken me regardless. Because they love children. Uncle Law said they told him over the phone they'd take me. Sight unseen, they took me."

Alan brightened as he listened.

Rusty went on earnestly, "You don't think they'd have taken a red-haired baby—a baby with carroty red hair—if they didn't love children?"

At that Alan's eyebrows rose. "Hey, you mean you're still bugged about your hair?"

"Well—no—not much any more," she realized. She added, "But there are still the freckles." She pivoted toward the mirror as if for confirmation. She leaned closer, wondering if she only imagined that her freckles were no longer so noticeable. Maybe missing out on swimming and other outdoor things at the lake last summer had lightened them.

Alan said, "There are actresses with freckles, you dope. If they got to be stars with freckles, what's your problem?"

She giggled, and looked again at the clock. "I'll be back," she assured him, grabbing a sweater to toss over her shoulders.

She skipped lightly down the stairs. A boy would go down *clumpety-clump*. That was hard on carpeting. On uncarpeted stairs it was hard on the ears. It was wonderfully strange, or strangely wonderful, this difference in boys and girls.

Standing just inside the door, watching for Sammy where it would not be too obvious that she was waiting for him, she decided that there really was a need for the light touch. There was a need for girls. It was hard to imagine that she could ever have thought that being a boy would be nicer than being a girl.

This time Sammy walked up the steps and put the paper in her hands, and he stopped long enough to comment on the fact that in a few days they would be going back to school.

Strangely enough, she was glad the holidays were almost over. It would be good to be back in school again, seeing and hearing all the kids. There would be so much to hear about and to tell about.

On the morning of their return to school, Alan hurried out of the house early, and Rusty was sure this must have something to do with the fact that his homework was properly done. She felt proud of him, and of herself.

As she neared the school, walking alone, she was puzzled at the sight of a number of boys carrying signs. The first sign she saw read UNFAIR TO CARVER. As she pondered the meaning of this, another sign moved close enough for her to see the words.

WE NEED EASTMAN, the crudely painted letters proclaimed.

She saw others, held aloft on slim sticks. DON'T FIRE EASTMAN. SAVE OUR COACH. WE PROTEST FIRING.

In her bewilderment, Rusty's footsteps halted. Then she was propelled forward by boys and girls around her. She heard excited questions —questions that made her heart quake and her knees shake. They were asking what the signs meant. She too wanted to know what the signs meant. She, even more than the others, wanted to know what this was all about.

Signs and Tears

THE SCHOOL BUZZED with excitement and indignation. Both boys and girls stopped Rusty to express their feelings. Some said they were sorry. Others said it just had to be a mistake. They said it wasn't possible for such a thing to happen at Carver High. "It's not fair," the girl friend of the president of the Student Council declared. "We'll have to hold a protest meeting. It's just not fair."

"You're darn right it's not fair," a boy standing behind her said wrathfully. "If anyone should be fired, it's the one who came up with this cockeyed idea of firing our coach."

"Yeah!" another boy shouted. "That's the one to fire! The guy who wants to fire our coach."

Rusty yearned to crawl into her locker and hide. It couldn't be true about her father. Yet, on the other hand, all this wouldn't be happening if the school weren't going to fire him, could it? All the while she was cold with fear that Alan might be involved in the demonstration. She had told him their father might lose his job. Alan had said he'd have to do something about it. Was this his idea of doing something about it? Were the signs his idea? She didn't want to believe that. Yet neither did she want to believe that her father was about to lose his job.

Just before the first bell rang for the lunch period, the teacher at the desk in her homeroom, Mr. Marvin, called for attention in order to read aloud an announcement from the principal's office. As Mr. Marvin started to read, Rusty's heart pounded so hard she could scarcely hear. Mr. Marvin was mentioning the signs.

"This is it," she thought. "They're going to lower the boom on somebody." Her father? Alan? The kids who'd carried the signs?

Mr. Marvin continued reading: "Our coach, Carl Eastman, has done an outstanding job ever since he joined our staff, and there are no plans whatsoever for letting him go."

There was loud clapping, and those near Rusty reached over to pat her back or shake her hand. Someone yelled, "Three cheers for our coach!"

Before Mr. Marvin's hand was fully raised in protest, the room began to rock to the sound of "Eastman! Eastman! Eastman! Yea! Yea! Yea!"

This demonstration for her father pleased Rusty. At the same time she was deeply disturbed, for now she was sure that Alan was responsible for the signs. He'd insisted when she was helping him with his school assignments that he must "see some of the guys" about something important. That important thing must have been the making of the signs. He had talked somebody into making them, and into carrying them around the school. Alan himself hadn't carried a sign, though.

But there would have been no signs if she had not led Alan to believe that their father might be fired. So all this was as much her fault as his. And what would happen when the school found out that it was the coach's own children who were responsible for this uproar?

During the lunch hour it seemed that everyone in school wanted to tell her how glad they were that the report about her father wasn't true. Everyone was being so nice, she was sure she just couldn't stand it. Time and again she thought she was going to blubber like a baby. She was grateful to Dawn, who stayed close and helped by speaking for her when she choked up and couldn't come out with more than a single "Thanks."

Maybe Dawn wouldn't be so nice to her if she knew, Rusty told herself dolefully. If Dawn learned who was responsible for what had happened, maybe Dawn wouldn't want to be friends with her any more.

When the dismissal bell finally rang, she pushed her way to her locker and then out of the building as quickly as possible. She kept her head down to avoid having to speak to anyone, and she walked faster and faster until she was all but running. Home had never seemed quite so far away, or so desirable.

Her mother was there, waiting. Rusty saw at once that her mother knew. "Your father phoned to tell me," her mother said, "so I wouldn't worry in case I heard about the signs."

Rusty dropped her books on the nearest chair and started to cry. At once her mother's arms were about her. Not since she and her parents had talked about her adoption had she sought refuge in her mother's arms. The boys didn't, and so it hadn't seemed a right thing for her to do. Now it seemed not only right but necessary.

When at last she was calmer, her mother helped take off her coat, and they sat side by side on the long sofa as Rusty confessed her part in what had happened. "If I hadn't tried to trick Alan into getting back on the team," she declared penitently, "he would never have done what he did."

Her mother's words were regretful but firm. "What you did wasn't right. If we said it was all right because you were doing it to help Alan, than we'd have to say what Alan did was all right because he thought he was helping his father."

Rusty sighed. "But Alan shouldn't get all the blame. If they find out at school, he will."

"I know. This may be pretty hard on Alan. He might want to shift all the blame on you. I think you should be prepared for that. Alan has never learned to take blame. Maybe now he'll have to."

Again Rusty sighed. "Maybe that's partly my fault, too." For hadn't she shielded him when she probably shouldn't have? She'd done it because she loved him. But that wasn't a good enough reason.

Her mother said, "Helping Alan with his schoolwork is quite another matter. That is being truly helpful. We're proud of you for it."

This brought forth more tears. But not tears of misery this time. And this time Rusty didn't care that her nose was getting all stuffed and her eyes would be like a couple of boiled onions. Even the unhappiness inside her felt good for a little while, with her mother's arms about her.

Taking the Blame

Rusty was alone in the house when Alan arrived home. Her mother had gone to pick up the other boys at school and take them to have their hair cut.

Because she wanted to make up for doing wrong, she had offered to take charge of the dinner. She browned serving-size pieces of spareribs, placed them in a shallow baking pan, and covered them with barbecue sauce. Potatoes were scrubbed, ready to bake. She was shredding cabbage for cole slaw when Alan came storming into the kitchen.

"*Sister!*" He spat out the word angrily. "Some sister you are! You sure made me look like a fool today!"

She held her tongue, waiting for him to calm down a little.

Alan ranted on. "My worst enemy couldn't have done a better job of knifing me in the back. If you were really my sister, you would never have done such a thing."

That hurt, but she pressed her lips together and went on grating the cabbage as Alan found more ways of expressing his anger toward her.

At last she said, "I was wrong. I heard Mother and Dad talking about a coach who lost his job. The reason I lied and said they were worried about Dad's job was because I hoped you might help him have a winning team."

He looked angrier than ever. "So it was a plot. To trick me. If the guys snitch, I'll tell everybody you lied to me and I believed you. That will get me off the hook."

Her mother had been right. Alan was trying to put all the blame on her. She couldn't let him do it. For his own sake as well as hers she couldn't let him do it. Somehow she managed to speak calmly. "Alan, you're just going to have to face up to things. You can't expect to get by on charm all your life. Why don't you make Mother and Dad proud of you by buckling down and—"

He started to bolt from the room as she spoke, but halted to shout at her, "Miss Know-It-All!

Why don't *you* start an advice column? But
first try to figure out why you can't catch a boy.
Let me tell you, you'll never catch Sammy by
waiting for him at the door every day. That's
not the way to—"

"Listen to who's talking!" she shouted back.
"I can't see that your method is getting you
anywhere with Dawn Borden!"

She saw that this had hit where it hurt. Immediately she was sorry, and she started to say
so, but Alan barged toward the stairs and his
room. She finished grating the cabbage and
started on a green pepper. Her hands were
shaking. So was she. It was hard to believe that
once upon a time she had enjoyed battling with
Alan. But their old battles, though they had
seemed important at the time, had never been
over anything of real consequence. This one
was different, and she shivered, worrying over
every word she'd said and its possible effect on
Alan.

She was still fretting when her father arrived
home. He asked, "Where is Alan?"

"In his room," she answered meekly.

Her father must know about Alan. Or sus-
pect. Otherwise he wouldn't look so stern.
Though she didn't want to, she forced herself to
confess to her father her part in what Alan had
done.

Mr. Eastman listened gravely without comment, then went upstairs.

When he came down he still looked grave, and also tired. "Alan," he said, "will have to tell his story to Mr. Otis. I doubt that Mr. Otis will think it necessary for you to be there."

Rusty hoped not. The high-school principal had always been most cordial to her. He was cordial because she was a member of the Eastman family, of course. She didn't want to change his attitude toward her. The very thought of an interview with Mr. Otis gave her goose bumps.

She welcomed the sound of the station wagon in the driveway and the noisy presence of the boys with their clipped hair fragrant with barber lotion. The boys had somehow heard about signs being carried around the high school that morning, and were full of comments and questions. "Just like a strike or something!" Peter exclaimed.

"Or a revolution," Gordon marveled. "That would be neat: a revolution in Melville."

At dinner that night Paul said wistfully, "I wish I'd been there. I'd have carried a sign for you, Dad."

"Well, thanks, Paul," his father said. "But under the circumstances there wouldn't have

been much point to it since there wasn't any
truth in the charge."

The boys went on talking. Their mother tried
to change the subject. "Your dinner is delicious,
Rusty. Isn't Rusty getting to be an excellent
cook?"

Gordon stopped chewing. "You mean Rusty
cooked this?"

The twins immediately joined in the teasing.
"Are you sure it's safe for us to eat?" Paul asked,
and Peter said, "What's the emergency phone
number, just in case?"

Rusty welcomed the laughter. Alan didn't
join in, she noticed. He didn't eat as much as
usual, and as soon as he'd finished his baked
apple he excused himself from the table. She
was sitting where she could see the mirror over
the dining-room buffet, and she saw that Alan
picked up his schoolbooks before heading up to
his room. If he was studying, as she hoped he
was, she wanted to help him.

When she and her mother were alone in the
kitchen, she mentioned this. Her mother put
an arm about her. "Maybe later he'll want you
to help. Right now I think it's better this way."

The words were no comfort. But the arm
about her was.

Sister to Brother

UNDOUBTEDLY HER MOTHER WAS RIGHT. But how much longer could she wait for Alan to think things-out for himself? With each passing day Rusty felt more and more miserable.

Because Alan had said it wasn't the smart thing to do, she decided that she would no longer wait at the door for Sammy and the afternoon paper. Sometimes she did peek through the window, being careful not to let Sammy see her. And sometimes it seemed to her that Sammy looked questioningly at the house, as if wondering why she didn't come out. Maybe she only imagined this, but it gave her some slight comfort.

She wished she could talk to Sammy about Alan. And she wished she could talk to Alan about Sammy. Especially about some of the

things Sammy had said. Sammy was very bright.
Brilliant was a better word for him. Alan certainly wasn't brilliant. But Alan could shine at
athletics, if he only would.

As the days continued to follow one another,
and Sammy made no effort to talk to her—
really talk to her, the way other boys did with
girls they liked—she came to the conclusion
that about this one thing Alan was right. Even
though Sammy had told her in so many words
that she was a very nice girl, this probably
didn't mean he really liked her. It was a most
discouraging conclusion to arrive at.

Sometimes she wished she had paid no attention to Alan's advice. If she hadn't listened to
him, she could still wait for Sammy and the
paper, and maybe he'd ask her for a date. Now
she would feel as if she were asking Sammy
for a date if she went out to get the paper. Listening to Alan had made her uncomfortable
and self-conscious whenever and wherever she
saw Sammy.

Just the same, she forgave Alan. Even though
she'd probably forgiven him seventy times
seven already, the way it said in the Bible, she
forgave him again.

Then one day, coming out of school, she saw
Alan look at Dawn. It was a defeated look,

and Rusty couldn't bear to see Alan look that way, not even about a girl.

He took his schoolbooks to the rec room these days, and he seemed to be trying hard to study. Whether he was trying for better grades, or just the privilege of driving the car, Rusty couldn't be sure. He no longer scowled at the sight of her, the way he had at first after that awful business at school. But he certainly showed no sign of welcoming her as she edged her way around the Ping-pong table which he was using as a desk.

She had planned her words carefully, but at the last minute they wanted to stick in her throat. She forced them out. "There's something I should have told you about Dawn."

He looked up, then down again quickly, but not before she saw the glint of hope in his eyes. "What about her?" Alan asked gruffly.

"I'm sure she likes you."

That brought a snort of disbelief. "Oh, yeah? Sure, she likes everybody."

"But she'd like you more," Rusty persisted, "if you'd just be yourself. Not all that smoothy talk. She likes people to be natural. She said so."

The stool Alan was perched on toppled over as he got angrily to his feet. "You mean you discussed me with Dawn? You mean you—"

"No, no, not really," Rusty hastened to assure him. "When she said that about being natural, it wasn't about you. We were talking about a girl. About Debra Damon, if you must know."

Alan looked relieved and disappointed at the same time. "So what's that got to do with me?"

"It's just that I can tell from the little things Dawn says. . . ." She paused, then stated positively, "A girl can tell," and was amazed at her own words. Yet it was true. She did know.

Alan straightened the stool and sat down, and she pulled up another stool and sat beside him. It seemed wise not to say too much about Dawn, so she quoted Sammy. "Sammy says not everyone should be expected to be an atomic scientist. But don't you think we all should do the things we are capable of doing? If we have talents, shouldn't we use them? Not just so we can be proud of ourselves. But it makes other people proud to know us."

When he started to protest, she said, "You've probably never realized how proud I've always been of you. I wanted to do all the things you did, even though I couldn't do them as well as you could. And now I'm not supposed to do them because I'm a girl. But I still want to be proud of you, Alan. And I think Dawn would feel that way too."

He kept his eyes on his schoolbooks. He

spoke slowly. "I don't know if I really believed it when you said Dad might lose his job. I guess maybe I just wanted to do something on my own and get credit for it. Credit for myself."

He didn't add, "Not as the coach's son." But Rusty knew that was what he meant. Her heart, which had started to rise with hope, began to sink.

"But—but—" she sputtered as she struggled for some way of making Alan see what she wanted him to see about himself. She spoke once again of Dawn. "I'm sure it doesn't matter one way or the other to Dawn that you're the coach's son. With Dawn, what counts is performance."

He started to smile, then frowned. "I suppose you mean I should put up or shut up."

"Well, after all, you haven't given Dawn much chance to see you in action, have you? She admires people who do things well. She—"

"All right, all right!" Alan cried out impatiently. "I get the message. So it's back to the muscle factory for me."

Rusty scarcely dared to believe her ears. "You mean it? You mean you'll get back on the team?"

Alan grinned. He looked happy—happier than she'd seen him look in a long while—as he cracked, "You mean I have a choice?"

Now it was her stool that toppled over. She flung her arms about Alan. She wanted to kiss him, but she didn't quite dare. "Oh, Alan!" she squealed.

"Hey!" he yelped. "I'm your brother, remember? Save that hugging stuff for Sammy or somebody."

The thought of Sammy dampened her spirits a little. But only a little. If things were going to work out for Alan, then why shouldn't they work out for her—and Sammy?

Swinging Alone

NEVER HAD A DAY been so bright and shining, of that Rusty was sure. The fact that the sun had not so much as peeked down at the earth all day didn't matter. Nor did it matter that there were a few puddles left over from yesterday's spring showers.

What mattered was that today was the day Alan, along with other boys at Carver, would be going out to the baseball diamond in the fenced-in area behind the school for the first practice session of the season. It no longer was important that he hadn't gone out for football or basketball. Today was what was significant.

She hurried out of school after the last bell, to pick a good spot from which to peer through the heavy wire-mesh fence. The team had not yet come out. As she waited she thought of Alan, wondering how he felt on this most important day.

She almost envied him. Almost, but not quite —for now she knew that she didn't have to give up all sports in order to be a proper young lady. What she really wanted was to be in a position similar to Alan's. Not on a baseball team, but doing something that demanded more of her than the ordinary things she did every day. Alan didn't know how lucky he was.

To her surprise, she was joined by Debra Damon. Rusty no longer disliked Debra. She wasn't especially fond of her, but she didn't dislike her.

A sudden breeze threatened to disarrange Debra's black hair, which hung almost straight to the tips of her ears, where it was supposed to turn under smoothly. Snatching at her wind-blown locks, Debra said, "Lucky you, with your curly hair. I envy you, Rusty, and that's a fact."

Whether or not it was a fact, Rusty was grateful to Debra. Compliments were good for the ego, and she told herself she must remember that other people probably felt the need of a boost to the ego now and then. Even Debra, unlikely though it once had seemed.

Debra said, "Isn't it great that Alan is going to play baseball again?"

"Great," Rusty agreed heartily.

"Will he pitch or play shortstop?"

"I don't know," Rusty admitted. "It all depends on where they need him most, I guess."

"Too bad he isn't twins," Debra said, giggling. "Then he could throw that slow ball of his and scoop it up in the infield, if the batter got a piece of it."

Rusty's mouth opened wide. She hadn't supposed Debra knew the difference between an infield fly and a home run.

Debra laughed. "Don't look so surprised. It helps with the boys to know a little about some of the things they know a lot about."

Just then a boy came along and tapped Debra on the shoulder. Apparently this boy was not interested in baseball, for he took Debra's hand and led her away, gazing into her eyes as if otherwise he'd surely lose his bearings.

Watching them, Rusty wondered once again if she had been right in taking Alan's advice about Sammy. Alan hadn't offered it as advice, of course; it had been given in angry criticism. Though she sometimes weakened and peeked at Sammy from behind the living-room draperies, she had stuck to her resolution not to be a boy chaser.

It was not only for her own sake that she did this. It was also for Alan's. How could she do less, now that Alan was following her advice with Dawn? So far, Dawn had dated Alan only a few times, bowling with other couples.

It was a start. Just as getting Alan back on the team was a start.

Some of the members of last year's team were coming on the field now, and there, with them, was Alan. Rusty let out a yell, "Yea, team!"

She thrilled as the cry was taken up and repeated by other watchers. At last things were going to be as they should be with Alan. He was really trying now. It wasn't going to be like a fairy tale, with everybody living happily ever after, any more than forever after she could forget that she was adopted and never wonder about her natural parents. But now she knew she was one of the lucky ones. "The chosen one," Alan had called her. But because she was chosen didn't mean she had no obligations toward those who had chosen her. Uncle Law had helped her to see why she was lucky. She had a family to love—a family to love her.

She watched Alan warming up, throwing the ball to one of last season's catchers.

From behind her a familiar voice said, "I figured you'd be here, Rusty." It was Jeri, looking as triumphant as if she'd just given the right answer on a quiz program. Rusty greeted her:

"Hi, Jeri, welcome to the fan club."

"Oh, I'm not a baseball fan," Jeri said with a shake of her blond hair. "I just came to do my good deed for the day."

Rusty was aware once again that Jeri was no longer the shy miss who had been her faithful friend in junior high.

From behind Jeri came another familiar voice. Rusty could scarcely believe her eyes: it was Sammy, brushing Jeri aside. "Jeri offered to help me find you," Sammy said. "As usual I'm in a hurry, but there's something I want to talk to you about."

Now it was her ears that Rusty could scarcely believe. "Well," she said weakly, "here I am."

"I know." Sammy grinned. "But I can't hang around to explain. I wondered—would you walk part way with me, Rusty, so we can talk?"

For just a moment sne was angry. She wanted to ask why he should be in such a hurry to talk to her all of a sudden, wnen for so long she'd been knocking herself out trying not to like him so much, and not to mind that he didn't stop her in the halls to talk to her the way other boys talked to girls they liked. She didn't expect him to hold her hand from classroom to classroom, the way some kids did. But he could have talked to her once in a while.

She started to say that she wanted to watch Alan and the team.

Sammy smiled again, and he had the kind of smile that said more than many words. "I want to tell you about a summer job," he explained.

"One for you and one for me. I can call you up when I finish delivering my papers, but I thought you might like to hear part of it now so you can be considering it."

It didn't make sense. A summer job? For her? For him? Even though she couldn't quite believe it, she walked with him, Alan forgotten. It took a little doing to get in step with Sammy. His step was long and his stride was swift. They were really swinging along as Sammy spoke with enthusiasm. "You know Miss Rosemary, who directs the Children's Community Theater." It was a statement, not a question.

"Of course. I worked on scenes and stuff. I never missed a play." It had been exciting, even if she hadn't been chosen for a part in the plays. Even if Debra had gotten the one part she'd wanted for herself.

"Well," Sammy said, still smiling, "the park district has decided to have a big recreation program for children this summer, with Miss Rosemary in charge. Part of it will be sports activities for the kids, and they need some junior helpers. I'm to be one. I told them you were good with kids and at all kinds of sports, and Miss Rosemary said she remembered you and she knew you would be a big help. So I'm quite sure you can have the job, if you want it."

Just a little while ago she had been scoffing

at fairy-tale endings. Yet if this wasn't a fairy tale, what was it? Maybe an answer to prayer? Rusty was so thrilled she could scarcely speak coherently. She hoped Sammy wouldn't think it was because her wind was bad. From what he'd said, she would need to be sound of both wind and limb to do this job well.

When they came to the corner where they had to turn in separate directions, he said, "Sorry I can't walk you home."

"That's all right," she said. "I know the way."

His eyes sparkled approval of her answer. "I'll call you tonight. If you'd like?"

"I'd like," she agreed promptly.

He started to leave, only to stop and say, "Maybe you could come outside for your paper the way you used to? I've missed that."

Her heart started acting like a string of Fourth of July firecrackers. Just in time she remembered Alan's advice. "Maybe," she said. "But be sure to call me. I can hardly wait to hear more."

That was putting it mildly, she told herself as she watched Sammy break into a sprint. He should be on the track team, she thought proudly. He probably would be, if he didn't need his job.

Greetings from homeward-bound boys and girls brought the realization that she was stand-

ing at the corner instead of turning toward
home. It was surprising how many of those who
passed knew her now, and spoke to her. True,
she was the coach's daughter. But before she
finished this school they would know her as
that and more, Rusty was sure.

Her summer job would be just the beginning.
It was tailor-made for her, she knew. As
Sammy had said, she was good at sports, and
she was good with little kids. It probably
wouldn't pay much. She would probably be an
assistant to an assistant to an assistant. That
didn't matter. It was going to be fun. And
Sammy would be there, which would make it
even more fun.

This time Miss Rosemary hadn't chosen
Debra. This time Rusty had been the chosen
one. She was glad she hadn't disliked Debra for
a long while now. Maybe she'd never really
hated her. Maybe she'd been envious. Whatever it had been, it wasn't part of her any more.

Suddenly it occurred to her that working out
in the sun all summer would probably start her
freckles popping like corn. Well, she could bear
it. She guessed there were worse things than
freckles a girl could have.

She wanted to skip. She wanted to dance.
She even wished she could sing loud as a brass
band as she went swinging along toward home.